I0651695

Harriet Martineau

**The Billow and the Rock**

A tale

Harriet Martineau

**The Billow and the Rock**
*A tale*

ISBN/EAN: 9783337174170

Printed in Europe, USA, Canada, Australia, Japan

Cover: Foto ©Andreas Hilbeck / pixelio.de

More available books at **www.hansebooks.com**

# THE
# BILLOW AND THE ROCK

## A Tale

BY

## HARRIET MARTINEAU

WITH
TWENTY-FOUR ILLUSTRATIONS BY E. J. WHEELER

LONDON
## GEORGE ROUTLEDGE AND SONS
BROADWAY, LUDGATE HILL
GLASGOW AND NEW YORK
1889

# NOTE.

*It is scarcely necessary to explain that in this tale free use has been made of the history of Lady Grange, whose name and adventures are probably familiar to many of my readers.*

# CONTENTS.

# THE
# BILLOW AND THE ROCK.

———◆◆———

## CHAPTER I.

### LORD AND LADY CARSE.

SCOTLAND was a strange and uncomfortable country to live
in a hundred years ago. Strange beyond measure its state
of society appears to us when we consider, not only that it
was called a Christian country, but that the people had
shown that they really did care very much for their religion,
and were bent upon worshipping God according to their
conscience and true belief. Whilst earnest in their religion,
their state of society was yet very wicked: a thing which
usually happens when a whole people are passing from one
way of living and being governed to another. Scotland had
not long been united with England. While the wisest of
the nation saw that the only hope for the country was in
being governed by the same king and parliament as the
English, many of the most powerful men wished not to be
governed at all, but to be altogether despotic over their
dependents and neighbours, and to have their own way in

everything. These lords and gentlemen did such violent things as are never heard of now in civilised countries; and when their inferiors had any strong desire or passion, they followed the example of the great men, so that travelling was dangerous; citizens did not feel themselves safe in their own houses if they had reason to believe they had enemies; few had any trust in the protection of the law; and stories of fighting and murder were familiar to children living in the heart of cities.

Children, however, had less liberty tnen than in our time. The more self-will there was in grown people, the more strictly were the children kept in order, not only because the uppermost idea of everyone in authority was that he would be obeyed, but because it would not do to let little people see the mischief that was going on abroad. So, while boys had their hair powdered, and wore long coats and waistcoats, and little knee-breeches, and girls were laced tight in stays all stiff with whalebone, they were trained to manners more formal than are ever seen now.

One autumn afternoon a party was expected at the house of Lord Carse, in Edinburgh; a handsome house in a very odd situation, according to our modern notions. It was at the bottom of a narrow lane of houses—that sort of lane called a Wynd in Scotch cities. It had a court-yard in front. It was necessary to have a court-yard to a good house in a street too narrow for carriages. Visitors must come in sedan chairs, and there must be some place, aside from the street, where the chairs and chairmen could wait for the guests. This old fashioned house had sitting-rooms on the ground floor, and on the sills of the windows were flower-pots, in which, on this occasion, some asters and other autumn flowers were growing.

Within the largest sitting-room was collected a formal group, awaiting the arrival of visitors. Lord Carse's sister, Lady Rachel Ballino, was there, surrounded by her nephews and nieces. As they came in, one after another, dressed for company, and made their bow or curtsey at the door, their aunt gave them permission to sit down till the arrival of the first guest, after which time it would be a matter of course that they should stand. Miss Janet and her brothers sat down on their low stools, at some distance from each other; but little Miss Flora had no notion of submitting to their restraints at her early age, and she scrambled up the window-seat to look abroad as far as she could, which was through the high iron gates to the tall houses on the other side the Wynd.

Lady Rachel saw the boys and Janet looking at each other with smiles, and this turned her attention to the child in the window, who was nodding her little curly head very energetically to somebody outside.

"Come down, Flora," said her aunt.

But Flora was too busy, nodding, to hear that she was spoken to.

"Flora, come down. Why are you nodding in that way?"

" Lady nods," said Flora.

Lady Rachel rose deliberately from her seat, and approached the window, turning pale as she went. After a single glance in the court-yard, she sank on a chair, and desired her nephew Orme to ring the bell twice. Orme, who saw that something was the matter, rang so vigorously as to bring the butler in immediately.

"John, you see?" said the pale lips of Lady Rachel, while she pointed, with a trembling finger, to the court-yard.

" Yes, my lady; the doors are fastened."

" And Lord Carse not home yet?"

" No, my lady. I think perhaps he is somewhere near, and cannot get home."

John looked irresolutely towards the child in the window. Once more Flora was desired to come down, and once more she only replied,

" Lady nods at me."

Janet was going towards the window to enforce her aunt's orders, but she was desired to keep her seat, and John quickly took up Miss Flora in his arms and set her down at her aunt's knee. The child cried and struggled, said she would see the lady, and must infallibly have been dismissed to the nursery, but her eye was caught, and her mind presently engaged by Lady Rachel's painted fan, on which there was a burning mountain, and a blue sea, and a shepherdess and her lamb—all very gay. Flora was allowed to have the fan in her own hands—a very rare favour. But presently she left off telling her aunt what she saw upon it, dropped it, and clapped her hands, saying, as she looked at the window, " Lady nods at me."

"JOHN, YOU SEE?" SAID THE PALE LIPS OF LADY RACHEL, WHILE SHE POINTED WITH A TREMBLING FINGER.

"It is mamma!" cried the elder ones, starting to their feet, as the lady thrust her face through the flowers, and close to the window-pane.

"Go to the nursery, children," said Lady Rachel, making an effort to rise. "I will send for you presently." The elder ones appeared glad to escape, and they carried with them the struggling Flora.

Lady Rachel threw up the sash, crossed her arms, and said, in the most formal manner,

"What do you want, Lady Carse?"

"I want my children."

"You cannot have them, as you well know. It is too late. I pity you; but it is too late."

"I will see my children. I will come home and live. I will make that tyrant repent setting up anyone in my place at home. I have it in my power to ruin him. I——"

"Abstain from threats," said Lady Rachel, shutting the window, and fastening the sash.

Lady Carse doubled her fist, as if about to dash in a pane; but the iron gates behind her creaked on their hinges, and she turned her head. A chair was entering, on each side of which walked a footman, whose livery Lady Carse well knew. Her handsome face, red before, was now more flushed. She put her mouth close to the window, and said, "If it had been anybody but Lovat you would not have been rid of me this evening. I would have stood among the chairmen till midnight for the chance of getting in. Be sure I shall to-morrow, or some day. But now I am off." She darted past the chair, her face turned away, just as Lord Lovat was issuing from it.

"Ho! ho!" cried he, in a loud and mocking tone. "Ho, there! my Lady Carse! A word with you!" But she ran up the Wynd as fast as she could go.

"You should not look so white upon it," Lord Lovat

A CHAIR WAS ENTERING.

observed to Lady Rachel, as soon as the door was shut. "Why do you let her see her power over you?"

"God knows!" replied Lady Rachel. "But it is not her threats alone that make us nervous. It is the being incessantly subject——"

She cleared her throat; but she could not go on.

Lord Lovat swore that he would not submit to be tormented by a virago in this way. If Lady Carse were his wife——

"Well! what would you do?" asked Lady Rachel.

"I would get rid of her. I tell your brother so. I would get rid of her in one way, if she threatened to get rid of me in another. She may have learned from her father how to put her enemies out of the way."

Lady Rachel grew paler than ever. Lord Lovat went on.

"Her father carried pistols in the streets of Edinburgh; and so may she. Her father was hanged for it; and it is my belief that she would have no objection to that end if she could have her revenge first. Ay! you wonder why I say such things to you, frightened as you are already. I do it that you may not infuse any weakness into your brother's purposes, if he should think fit to rid the town of her one of these days. Come, come! I did not say rid the world of her."

"Merciful Heaven! no!"

"There are places, you know, where troublesome people have no means of doing mischief. I could point out such a place presently, if I were asked—a place where she might be as safe as under lock and key, without the trouble and risk of confining her, and having to consider the law."

"You do not mean a prison, then?"

"No. She has not yet done anything to make it easy to put her in prison for life; and anything short of that would be more risk than comfort. If Carse gives me authority, I will dispose of her where she can be free to rove like the wild goats. If she should take a fancy to jump down a precipice, or drown herself, that is her own affair, you know."

The door opened for the entrance of company. Lord Lovat whispered once more,

"Only this. If Carse thinks of giving the case into my hands, don't you oppose it. I will not touch her life, I swear to you."

Lady Rachel knew, like the rest of the world, that Lord Lovat's swearing went for no more than any of his other engagements. Though she would have given all she had in the world to be freed from the terror of Lady Carse, and to hope that the children might forget their unhappy mother, she shrank from the idea of putting any person into the hands of the hard, and mocking, and plotting Lord Lovat. As for the legality of doing anything at all to Lady Carse while she did not herself break the law, that was a consideration which no more occurred to Lady Rachel than to the violent Lord Lovat himself.

Lady Rachel was exerting herself to entertain her guests, and had sent for the children, when, to her inexplicable relief, the butler brought her the news that Lord Carse and his son Willie were home, and would appear with all speed. They had been detained two hours in a tavern, John said.

"In a tavern?"

"Yes, my lady.  Could not get out.  Did not wish to collect more people, to cause a mob.  It is all right now, my lady."

When Lord Carse entered, he made formal apologies to his guests first, and his sister afterwards, for his late appearance.  He had been delayed by an affair of importance on his way home.  His rigid countenance was somewhat paler than usual, and his manner more dictatorial.  His hard and unwavering voice was heard all the evening, prosing and explaining.  The only tokens of feeling were when he spoke to his eldest son Willie, who was spiritless, and, as the close observer saw, tearful; and when he took little Flora in his arms, and stroked her shining hair, and asked her if she had been walking with the nurse.

Flora did not answer.  She was anxiously watching Lady Rachel's countenance.  Her papa bade her look at him and answer his question.  She did so, after glancing at her aunt, and saying eagerly, in a loud whisper,

"I am not going to say anything about the lady that came to the window, and nodded at me."

It did not mend the matter that her sister and brothers all said at once, in a loud whisper, "Hush ! Flora."

Her father sat her down hastily.  Lord Carse's domestic troubles were pretty well known throughout Edinburgh; and the company settled it in their own minds that there had been a scene this afternoon.

When they were gone, Lord Carse gave his sister his

advice not to instruct any very young child in any part to be acted. He assured her that very young children have not the discretion of grown people, and gave it as his opinion that when the simplicity, which is extremely agreeable by the domestic fireside, becomes troublesome or dangerous in society, the child is better disposed of in the nursery.

Lady Rachel meekly submitted; only observing what a singular and painful case was that of these children, who had to be so early trained to avoid the very mention of their mother. She believed her brother to be the most religious man she had ever known; yet she now heard him mutter oaths so terrible that they made her blood run cold.

"Brother! my dear brother," she expostulated.

"I'll tell you what she has done," he said, from behind his set teeth. "She has taken a lodging in this very Wynd, directly opposite my gates. Not a child, not a servant, not a dog or cat can leave my house without coming under her eye. She will be speaking to the children out of her window."

"She will be nodding at Flora from the court-yard as often as you are out," cried Lady Rachel. "And if she should shoot you from her window, brother."

"She hints that she will; and there are many things more unlikely, considering (as she herself says) whose daughter she is.—But, no," he continued, seeing the dreadful alarm into which his sister was thrown. "This will not be her method of revenge. There is another that pleases her better, because she suspects that I dread it more.—You know what I mean?"

"Political secrets?" Lady Rachel whispered—not in Flora's kind of whisper, but quite into her brother's ear.

He nodded assent, and then he gravely informed her that his acquaintance, Duncan Forbes, had sent a particular request to see him in the morning. He should go, he said. It would not do to refuse waiting on the President of the Court of Session, as he was known to be in Edinburgh. But he wished he was a hundred miles off, if he was to hear a Hanoverian lecture from a man so good natured, and so dignified by his office, that he must always have his own way.

Lady Rachel went to bed very miserable this night. She wished that Lady Carse and King George, and all the House of Brunswick had never existed; or that Prince Charlie, or some of the exiled royal family, would come over at once and take possession of the kingdom, that her brother and his friends might no longer be compelled to live in a state of suspicion and dread—every day planning to bring in a new king, and every day obliged to appear satisfied with the one they had; their secret, or some part of it, being all the while at the mercy of a violent woman who hated them all.

# CHAPTER II.

## THE TURBULENT.

WHEN Lord Carse issued from his own house the next morning to visit the President, he had his daughter Janet by his side, and John behind him. He took Janet in the hope that her presence, while it would be no impediment to any properly legal business, would secure him from any political conversation being introduced ; and there was no need of any apology for her visit, as the President usually asked why he had not the pleasure of seeing her, if her father went alone. Duncan Forbes's good nature to all young people was known to everybody ; but he declared himself an admirer of Janet above all others ; and Janet never felt herself of so much consequence as in the President's house. John went as an escort to his young lady on her return.

Janet felt her father's arm twitch as they issued from their gates ; and, looking up to see why, she saw that his face was twitching too. She did not know how near her mother was, nor that her father and John had their ears on the stretch for a hail from the voice they dreaded above all others in the world. But nothing was seen or heard of Lady Carse ; and when they turned out of the Wynd Lord Carse resumed his usual air and step of formal importance ; and Janet held up her head, and tried to take steps as long as his.

All was right about her going to the President's.  He kissed her forehead, and praised her father for bringing her, and picked out for her the prettiest flowers from a bouquet

JANET HELD UP HER HEAD AND TRIED TO TAKE STEPS
AS LONG AS HIS.

before he sat down to business; and then he rose again, and provided her with a portfolio of prints to amuse herself with; and even then he did not forget her, but glanced aside several times, to explain the subject of some print, or to draw her attention to some beauty in the one she was looking at.

"My dear lord," said he, "I have taken a liberty with your time; but I want your opinion on a scheme I have drawn out at length for Government, for preventing and punishing the use of tea among the common people."

"Very good, very good!" observed Lord Carse, greatly relieved about the reasons for his being sent for. "It is high time, if our agriculture is to be preserved, that the use of malt should be promoted to the utmost by those in power."

"I am sure of it," said the President. "Things have got to such a pass, that in towns the meanest people have tea at the morning's meal, to the discontinuance of the ale which ought to be their diet; and poor women drink this drug also in the afternoons, to the exclusion of the twopenny."

"It is very bad; very unpatriotic; very immoral," declared Lord Carse. "Such people must be dealt with outright."

The President put on his spectacles, and opened his papers to explain his plan—that plan, which it now appears almost incredible should have come from a man so wise, so liberal, so kind-hearted as Duncan Forbes. He showed how he would draw the line between those who ought and those who ought not to be permitted to drink tea; how each was to be described, and how, when anyone was suspected of taking tea, when he ought to be drinking beer, he was to tell on oath what his income was, that it might be judged whether he could pay the extremely high duty on tea which the plan would impose. Houses might be visited, and cupboards and cellars searched, at all hours, in cases of suspicion.

"These provisions are pretty severe," the President himself observed. "But——"

"But not more than is necessary," declared Lord Carse. "I should say they are too mild. If our agriculture is not supported, if the malt tax falls off, what is to become of us?"

And he sighed deeply.

"If we find this scheme work well, as far as it goes," observed the President, cheerfully, "we can easily render it as much more stringent as occasion may require. And now, what can Miss Janet tell us on this subject? Can she give information of any tea being drunk in the nursery at home?"

"Oh! to be sure," said Janet. "Nurse often lets me have some with her; and Katie fills Flora's doll's teapot out of her own, almost every afternoon."

"Bless my soul!" cried Lord Carse, starting from his seat in consternation. "My servants drink tea in my house! Off they shall go—every one of them who does it."

"Oh! papa. No; pray papa!" implored Janet. "They will say I sent them away. Oh! I wish nobody had asked me anything about it."

"It was my doing," said the President. "My dear lord, I make it my request that your servants may be forgiven."

Lord Carse bowed his acquiescence; but he shook his head, and looked very gloomy about such a thing happening in his house. The President agreed with him that it must not happen again, on pain of instant dismissal.

The President next invited Janet to the drawing-room to see a grey parrot, brought hither since her last visit—a very entertaining companion in the evenings, the President declared. He told Lord Carse he would be back in three minutes, and so he was—with a lady on his arm, and that lady was—Lady Carse.

She was not flushed now, nor angry, nor forward. She was quiet and ladylike, while in the house of one of the most gentlemanly men of his time. If her husband had looked at her, he would have seen her so much like the woman he wooed and once dearly loved, that he might have somewhat changed his feelings towards her. But he went abruptly to the window when he discovered who she was, and nothing could make him turn his head. Perhaps he was aware how pale he was, and desired that she should not see it.

The President placed the lady in a chair, and then approached Lord Carse, and laid his hand on his shoulder, saying,

"You will forgive me when you know my reasons. I want you to join me in prevailing on this good lady to give up a design which I think imprudent — I will say, wrong."

It was surprising, but Lady Carse for once bore quietly with somebody thinking her wrong. Whatever she might feel, she said nothing. The President went on.

"Lady Carse——"

He felt, as his hand lay on his friend's shoulder, that he winced, as if the very name stung him.

"Lady Carse," continued the President, "cannot be deterred by any account that can be given her of the perils and hardships of a journey to London. She declares her intention of going."

"I am no baby; I am no coward," declared the lady. "The coach would not have been set up, and it would not continue to go once a fortnight if the journey were not practicable; and where others go I can go."

"Of the dangers of the road, I tell this good lady," resumed the President, "she can judge as well as you or I, my lord. But of the perils of the rest of her errand she must, I think, admit that we may be better judges."

"How can you let your Hanoverian prejudices seduce you into countenancing such a devil as that woman, and believing a word that she says?" muttered Lord Carse, in a hoarse voice.

"Why, my good friend," replied the President, "it does so vex my very heart every day to see how the ladies, whom I would fain honour for their discretion as much as I admire them for their other virtues, are wild on behalf of the Pretender, or eager for a desperate and treasonable war, that you must not wonder if I take pleasure in meeting with one who is loyal to her rightful sovereign. Loyal, I must suppose, at home, and in a quiet way ; for she knows that I do not approve of her journey to London to see the minister.

"The minister!" faltered out Lord Carse.

He heard, or fancied he heard his wife laughing behind him.

"Come, now, my friends," said the President, with a good-humoured seriousness, "let me tell you that the position of either of you is no joke. It is too serious for any lightness and for any passion. I do not want to hear a word about your grievances. I see quite enough. I see a lady driven from home, deprived of her children, and tormenting herself with thoughts of revenge because she has no other object. I see a gentleman who has been cruelly put to shame in his own house and in the public street, worn with anxiety about his innocent daughters, and with natural fears—inevitable fears, of the mischief that may be done to his character and fortunes by an ill use of the confidence he once gave to the wife of his bosom."

There was a suppressed groan from Lord Carse, and something like a titter from the lady. The President went on even more gravely.

"I know how easy it is for people to make each other

wretched, and especially for you two to ruin each other. If I could but persuade you to sit down with me to a quiet discussion of a plan for living together or apart, abstaining from mutual injury——"

Lord Carse dissented audibly from their living together, and the lady from living apart.

"Why," remonstrated the President, "things cannot be worse than they are now. You make life a hell——"

"I am sure it is to me!" sighed Lord Carse.

"It is not yet so to me," said the lady. "I——"

"It is not!" thundered her husband, turning suddenly round upon her. "Then I will take care it shall be."

"For God's sake, hush!" exclaimed the President, shocked to the soul.

"Do your worst," said the lady, rising. "We will try which has the most power. You know what ruin is."

"Stop a moment," said the President. "I don't exactly like to have this quiet house of mine made a hell of. I cannot have you part on these terms."

But the lady had curtseyed, and was gone.

For a minute or two nothing was said. Then a sort of scream was heard from upstairs.

"My Janet!" cried Lord Carse.

"I will go and see," said the President. "Janet is my especial pet, you know."

He immediately returned, smiling, and said,

"There is nothing amiss with Janet. Come and see."

Janet was on her mother's lap, her arms thrown round her neck, while the mother's tears streamed over them

"CAN YOU RESIST THIS?" THE PRESIDENT ASKED OF LORD CARSE.

both. "Can you resist this?" the President asked of Lord Carse. "Can you keep them apart after this?"

"I can," he replied. "I will not permit her the devilish pleasure she wants—of making my own children my enemies."

He was going to take Janet by force: but the President interfered, and said authoritatively to Lady Carse that she had better go: her time was not yet come. She must wait; and his advice was to wait patiently and harmlessly.

It could not have been believed how instantaneously a woman in such emotion could recover herself.

She put Janet off her knee. In an instant there were no more traces of tears, and her face was composed, and her manner hard.

"Good-bye, my dear," she said to the weeping Janet. "Don't cry so, my dear. Keep your tears; for you will have something more to cry for soon. I am going home to pack my trunk for London. Have my friends any commands for London?"

And she looked round steadily upon the three faces.

The President was extremely grave when their eyes met; but even his eye sank under hers. He offered his arm to conduct her downstairs, and took leave of her at the gate with a silent bow.

He met Lord Carse and Janet coming downstairs, and begged them to stay awhile, dreading, perhaps, a street encounter. But Lord Carse was bent on being gone immediately—and had not another moment to spare.

# CHAPTER III.

## THE WRONG JOURNEY.

LADY CARSE and her maid Bessie—an elderly woman who had served her from her youth up, bearing with her temper for the sake of that family attachment which exists so strongly in Scotland, — were busy packing trunks this afternoon, when they were told that a gentleman must speak with Lady Carse below stairs.

"There will be no peace till we are off," observed the lady to her maid. In answer to which Bessie only sighed deeply.

"I want you to attend me downstairs," observed the lady. "But this provoking nonsense of yours, this crying about going a journey, has made you not fit to be seen. If any friend of my lord's saw your red eyes, he would go and say that my own maid was on my lord's side. I must go down alone."

"Pray, madam, let me attend you. The gentleman will not think of looking at me : and I will stand with my back to the light, and the room is dark."

"No ; your very voice is full of tears. Stay where you are."

Lady Carse sailed into the room very grandly, not knowing whom she was to see. Nor was she any wiser when she did see him. He was muffled up, and wore a shawl tied over his mouth, and kept his hat on; so that little space was left between hat, periwig, and comforter. He apologised for wearing his hat, and for keeping the lady standing—his business was short:—in the first place to show her Lord Carse's ring, which she would immediately recognise.

She glanced at the ring, and knew it at once.

"On the warrant of this ring," continued the gentleman, "I come from your husband to require from you what you cannot refuse,—either as a wife, or consistent with your safety. You hold a document,—a letter from your husband, written to you in conjugal confidence five years ago, from London,—a letter——"

"You need not describe it further," said the lady. "It is my chief treasure, and not likely to escape my recollection. It is a letter from Lord Carse, containing treasonable expressions relating to the royal family."

"About the treason we might differ, madam; but my business is, not to argue that, but to require of you to deliver up that paper to me, on this warrant," again producing the ring.

The lady laughed, and asked whether the gentleman was a fool or took her to be one, that he asked her to give up what she had just told him was the greatest treasure she had in the world,—her sure means of revenge upon her enemies.

" You will not ? " asked the gentleman.

" I will not."

LADY CARSE CAUGHT AT THE TABLE, AND LEANED ON IT TO
SUPPORT HERSELF.

" Then hear what you have to expect, madam. Hear it,
and then take time to consider once more."

" I have no time to spare," she replied. " I start for

3

London early in the morning; and my preparations are not complete."

"You must hear me, however," said the gentleman. "If you do not yield your husband will immediately and irrevocably put you to open shame."

"He cannot," she replied. "I have no shame. I have the advantage of him there."

"You have, however, personal liberty at present. You have that to lose,—and life, madam. You have that to lose."

Lady Carse caught at the table, and leaned on it to support herself. It was not from fear about her liberty or life; but because there was a cruel tone in the utterance of the last words, which told her that it was Lord Lovat who was threatening her; and she *was* afraid of him.

"I have shaken you now," said he. "Come: give me the letter."

"It is not fear that shakes me," she replied. "It is disgust. The disgust that some feel at reptiles I feel at you, my Lord Lovat."

She quickly turned and left the room. When he followed she had her foot on the stairs. He said aloud,

"You will repent, madam. You will repent."

"That is my own affair."

"True, madam, most true. I charge you to remember that you have yourself said that it is your own affair if you find you have cause to repent."

Lady Carse stood on the stairs till her visitor had closed the house door behind him, struggled up to her chamber, and fainted on the threshold.

"This journey will never do, madam," said Bessie, as her mistress revived.

"It is the very thing for me," protested the lady. "In twelve hours more we shall have left this town and my enemies behind us; and then I shall be happy."

Bessie sighed. Her mistress often talked of being happy; but nobody had ever yet seen her so.

"This fainting is nothing," said Lady Carse, rising from the bed. "It is only that my soul sickens when Lord Lovat comes near; and the visitor below was Lord Lovat."

"Mercy on us!" exclaimed Bessie. "What next?"

"Why, that we must get this lock turned," said her lady, kneeling on the lid of a trunk. "Now, try again. There it is! Give me the key. Get me a cup of tea, and then to bed with you! I have a letter to write. Call me at four, to a minute. Have you ordered two chairs, to save all risk?"

"Yes, madam; and the landlord will see your things to the coach office to-night."

Lady Carse had sealed her letter, and was winding up her watch with her eyes fixed on the decaying fire, when she was startled by a knock at the house door. Everybody else was in bed. In a vague fear she hastened to her chamber, and held the door in her hand and listened while the landlord went down. There were two voices besides his; and there was a noise as of something heavy brought into the hall. When this was done, and the bolts and bars were again fastened, she went to the stair head and saw the landlord coming up with a letter in his hand. The letter was for her. It was heavy. Her trunks had come back from the coach office. The London coach was gone.

The letter contained the money paid for the fare of Lady Carse and her maid to London, and explained that a person of importance having occasion to go to London with attendants, and it being necessary to use haste, the coach was compelled to start six hours earlier than usual; and Lady Carse would have the first choice of places next time;—that is in a fortnight.

Bessie had never seen her mistress in such a rage as now: and poor Bessie was never to see it again. At the first news, she was off her guard, and thanked Heaven that this dangerous journey was put off for a fortnight; and much might happen in that time. Her mistress turned round upon her, said it was not put off,—she would go on horseback alone,—she would go on foot,—she would crawl on her knees, sooner than give up. Bessie was silent, well knowing that none of these ways would or could be tried, and thankful that there was only this one coach to England. Enraged at her silence, her mistress declared that no one who was afraid to go to London was a proper servant for her, and turned her off upon the spot. She paid her wages to the weeping Bessie, and with the first light of morning, sent her from the house, herself closing the door behind her. She then went to bed, drawing the curtains close round it, remaining there all the next day, and refusing food.

In the evening, she wearily rose, and slowly dressed herself,—for the first time in her life without help. She was fretted and humbled at the little difficulties of her toilet, and secretly wished, many times, that Bessie would come back and offer her services, though she was resolved to appear not to accept them without a very humble apology from Bessie for her fears about London. At last, she was ready to go down to tea, dressed in a wrapping gown and slippers. When halfway down, she heard a step behind her, and looked round. A Highlander was just two stairs above her: another appeared at the foot of the flight; and more were in the hall. She knew the livery. It was Lovat's tartan.

They dragged her downstairs, and into her parlour, where she struggled so violently that she fell against the heavy table, and knocked out two teeth. They fastened down her arms by swathing her with a plaid, tied a cloth over her mouth, threw another over her head, and carried her to the door. In the street was a sedan chair; and in the chair was a man who took her upon his knees, and held her fast. Still she struggled so desperately, that the chair rocked from side to side, and would have been thrown over; but that there were plenty of attendants running along by the side of it, who kept it upright.

This did not last very long. When they had got out of the streets, the chair stopped. The cloth was removed from her head; and she saw that they were on the Linlithgow road, that some horsemen were waiting, one of whom was on a very stout horse, which bore a pillion behind the saddle. To this person she was formally introduced, and told that he was Mr. Forster of Corsebonny. She knew Mr. Forster to be a gentleman of character; and that therefore her personal safety was secure in his hands. But her good opinion of him determined her to complain and appeal to him in a way which she believed no gentleman could resist. She did not think of making any outcry. The party was large; the road was unfrequented at night; and she dreaded being gagged. She therefore only spoke,—and that as calmly as she could.

"What does this mean, Mr. Forster? Where are you carrying me?"

"I know little of Lord Carse's purposes, madam; and less of the meaning of them probably than yourself."

"My Lord Carse! Then I shall soon be among the dead. He will go through life with murder on his soul."

"You wrong him, madam. Your life is very safe."

"No; I will not live to be the sport of my husband's mercy. I tell you, sir, I will not live."

"Let me advise you to be silent, madam. Whatever we have to say will be better said at the end of our stage, where I hope you will enjoy good rest, under my word that you shall not be molested."

But the lady would not be silent. She declared very peremptorily her determination to destroy herself on the first opportunity; and no one who knew her temper could dispute the probability of her doing that, or any other act of passion. From bewailing herself, she went on to say things of her husband and Lord Lovat, and of her purposes in regard to them, which Mr. Forster felt that he and others ought not, for her own sake, to hear. He quickened his pace, but she complained of cramp in her side. He then halted, whispered to two men who watched for his orders, and had the poor lady again silenced by the cloth being tied over her mouth. She tried to drop off, but that only caused the strap which bound her to the rider to be buckled tighter. She found herself treated like a wayward child. When she could no longer make opposition, the pace of the party was quickened, and it was not more than two hours past midnight when they reached a country house, which she knew to belong to an Edinburgh lawyer, a friend of her husband's.

Servants were up—fires were burning—supper was on the table. The lady was shown to a comfortable bedroom.

From thence she refused to come down. Mr. Forster and another gentleman of the party therefore visited her to explain as much as they thought proper of Lord Carse's plans, and of their own method of proceeding.

They told her that Lord Carse found himself compelled, for family reasons, to sequestrate her. For her life and safety there was no fear; but she was to live where she could have that personal liberty of which no one wished to deprive her, without opportunity of intercourse with her family.

"And where can that be?" she asked. "Who will undertake to say that I shall live, in the first place, and that my children shall not hear from me, in the next?"

"Where your abode is to be, we do not know," replied Mr. Forster. "Perhaps it is not yet settled. As for your life, madam, I have engaged to transfer you alive and safe, as far as lies in human power."

"Transfer me! To whom?"

"To another friend of your husband's, who will take equal care of you. I am sorry for your threats of violence on yourself. They compel me to do what I should not otherwise have thought of—to forbid your being alone, even in this your own room."

"You do not mean——"

"I mean that you are not to be left unwatched for a single instant. There is a woman in the house—the housekeeper. She and her husband will enter this room when I leave it; and I advise you to say nothing to them against this arrangement."

" They shall have no peace with me."

" I am sorry for it. It will be a bad preparation for your further journey. You would do better to lie down and rest, —for which ample time shall be allowed."

The people in charge of the house were summoned, and ordered, in the lady's hearing, to watch her rest, and on no account to leave the room till desired to do so. A table was set out in one corner, with meat and bread, wine and ale. But the unhappy lady would not attempt either to eat or sleep. She sat by the fire, faint, weary and gloomy. She listened to the sounds from below till the whole party had supped, and lain down for the night. Then she watched her guards,—the woman knitting, and the man reading his Bible. At last, she could hold up no longer. Her head sank on her breast, and she was scarcely conscious of being gently lifted, laid upon the bed, and covered up warm with cloak and plaid.

# CHAPTER IV.

## NEWSPAPERS.

LADY CARSE did not awake till the afternoon of the next day; and then she saw the housekeeper sitting knitting on the same chair, and looking as if she had never stirred since she took her place there in the middle of the night. The man was not there.

The woman cheerfully invited the lady to rise and refresn herself, and come to the fire, and then go down and dine. But Lady Carse's spirit was awake as soon as her eyes were. She said she would never rise—never eat again. The woman begged her to think better of it, or she should be obliged to call her husband to resume his watch, and to let Mr. Forster know of her refusal to take food. To this the poor lady answered only by burying her face in the coverings, and remaining silent and motionless, for all the woman could say.

In a little while, up came Mr. Forster, with three High-landers. They lifted her, as if she had been a child, placed her in an easy chair by the fireside, held back her head, and poured down her throat a basin full of strong broth.

"It grieves me, madam," said Mr. Forster, "to be com-pelled to treat you thus—like a wayward child. But I am answerable for your life. You will be fed in this way as often as you decline necessary food."

"I defy you still," she cried.

"Indeed!" said he, with a perplexed look. She had been searched by the housekeeper in her sleep; and it was certain that no weapon and no drug was about her person. She presently lay back in the chair, as if wishing to sleep, throwing a shawl over her head; and all withdrew except the housekeeper and her husband.

In a little while some movement was perceived under the shawl, and there was a suppressed choking sound. The desperate woman was swallowing her hair, in order to vomit up the nourishment she had taken—as another lady in desperate circumstances once did to get rid of poison. The housekeeper was ordered to cut off her hair, and Mr. Forster then rather rejoiced in this proof that she carried no means of destroying her life.

As soon as it was quite dark she was compelled to take more food, and then wrapped up warmly for a night ride. Mr. Forster invited her to promise that she would not speak, that he might be spared the necessity of bandaging her mouth. But she declared her intention of speaking on every possible occasion; and she was therefore effectually prevented from opening her mouth at all.

On they rode through the night, stopping to dismount only twice; and then it was not at any house, but at mere sheepfolds, where a fire was kindled by some of the party, and where they drank whisky, and laughed and talked in the warmth and glow of the fire, as if the poor lady had not been present. Between her internal passion, her need of more food than she would take, the strangeness of the scene, with the sparkling cold stars overhead, and the heat and glow of the fire under the wall—amidst these distracting influences the lady felt confused and ill, and would have been glad now to have been free to converse quietly, and to accept the mercy Mr. Forster had been ready to show her. He was as watchful as ever, sat next her as she lay on the ground, said at last that they had not much further to go, and felt her pulse. As the grey light of morning strengthened, he went slower and slower, and encouraged her to lean upon him, which her weakness compelled her to do. He sent forward the factor of the estate they were now entering upon, desiring him to see that everything was warm and comfortable.

When the building they were approaching came in view, the poor lady wondered how it could ever be made warm and comfortable. It was a little old tower, the top of which was in ruins, and the rest as dreary looking as possible. Cold and bare it stood on a waste hill side. It would have looked like a mere grey pillar set down on the scanty pasture, but for a square patch behind, which was walled in by a hard ugly wall of stones. A thin grey smoke arose from it, showing that someone was within; and dogs began to bark as the party drew near.

One woman was here as at the last resting place. She showed the way by the narrow winding stair, up which Lady Carse was carried like a corpse, and laid on a little bed in a very small room, whose single window was boarded up,

HE ENCOURAGED HER TO LEAN UPON HIM.

leaving only a square of glass at the top to admit the light.

Mr. Forster stood at the bedside, and said firmly,

"Now, Lady Carse, listen to me for a moment, and then you will be left with such freedom as this room and this woman's attendance can afford you. You are so exhausted, that we have changed our plan of travel. You will remain here, in this room, till you have so recruited yourself by food and rest as to be able to proceed to a place where all restraint will be withdrawn. When you think yourself able to proceed, and declare your willingness to do so, I, or a friend of mine, will be at your service—at your call at any hour. Till then this room is your abode; and till then I bid you farewell."

He unfastened the bandage, and was gone before she could speak to him. What she wanted to say was, that on such terms she would never leave this room again. She desired the woman to tell him so; but the woman said she had orders to carry no messages.

Where there is no help and no hope, any force of mere temper is sure to give way, as Mr. Forster well knew. Injured people who have done no wrong, and who bear no anger against their enemies, have an inward strength and liberty of mind which enable them to bear on firmly, and to be immovable in their righteous purposes; so that, as has been shown by many examples, they will be torn limb from limb sooner than yield. Lady Carse was an injured person— most deeply injured, but she was not innocent. She had a purpose; but it was a vindictive one; and her soul was all tossed with passion, instead of being settled in patience. So her intentions of starving herself—of making Mr. Forster miserable by killing herself through want of sleep and food, gave way; and then she was in a rage with herself for having given way. When all was still in the tower, and

the silent woman who attended her knitted on for hours together, as if she was a machine ; and there was nothing to
be seen from the boarded window; and the smouldering
peats in the fireplace looked as if they were asleep, Lady
Carse could not always keep awake, and, once asleep, she
did not wake for many hours.

When, at length, she started up and looked around her,
she was alone, and the room was lighted only by a flickering
blaze from the fireplace.    This dancing light fell on a little
low round table, on which was a plate with some slices of
mutton-ham, some oatcake, three or four eggs, and a pitcher.
She was ravenously hungry, and she was alone.  She thought
she would take something—so little as to save her pride,
and not to show that she had yielded.   But, once yielding,
this was impossible.   She ate, and ate, till all was gone—
even the eggs ; and it would have been the same if they had
been raw.   The pitcher contained ale, and she emptied it.
When she had done, she could have died with shame.   She
was just thinking of setting her dress on fire, when she heard
the woman's step on the stair.   She threw herself on the
bed, and pretended to be asleep.   Presently she was so, and
she had another long nap.   When she woke the table had
nothing on it but the woman's knitting ; the woman was
putting peats on the fire, and she made no remark, then or
afterwards, on the disappearance of the food.   From that
day forward food was laid out while the lady slept; and
when she awoke, she found herself alone to eat it.   It was

served without knife or fork, with only bone spoons. It would have been intolerable shame to her if she had known that she was watched, through a little hole in the door, as a precaution against any attempt on her life.

But her intentions of this kind too gave way. She was well aware that though not free to go where she liked she could, any day, find herself in the open air with liberty to converse, except on certain subjects ; and that she might presently be in some abode—she did not know what— where she could have full personal liberty, and her present confinement being her own choice made it much less dignified, and this caused her to waver about throwing off life and captivity together. The moment never came when she was disposed to try.

At the end of a week she felt great curiosity to know whether Mr. Forster was at the tower all this time waiting her pleasure. She would not enquire lest she should be suspected of the truth—that she was beginning to wish to see him. She tried one or two distant questions on her attendant, but the woman knew nothing. There seemed to be no sort of question that she could answer.

In a few days more the desire for some conversation with somebody became very pressing, and Lady Carse was not in the habit of denying herself anything she wished for. Still, her pride pulled the other way. The plan she thought of was to sit apparently musing or asleep by the fire while her attendant swept the floor of her room, and suddenly to run downstairs while the door was open. This she did one day, when she was pretty sure she had heard an unusual sound of horses' feet below. If Mr. Forster should be going without her seeing him it would be dreadful. If he should have arrived after an absence this would afford a pretext for renewing intercourse with him. So she watched her moment, sprang to the door, and was down the stair before her attendant could utter a cry of warning to those below.

Lady Carse stood on the last stair, gazing into the little kitchen, which occupied the ground floor of the tower. Two or three people turned and gazed at her, as startled, perhaps, as herself; and she *was* startled, for one of them was Lord Lovat.

Mr. Forster recovered himself, bowed, and said that perhaps she found herself able to travel; in which case, he was at her service.

"O dear, no!" she said. She had no intention whatever of travelling further. She had heard an arrival of horsemen, and had merely come down to know if there was any news from Edinburgh.

Lord Lovat bowed, said he had just arrived from town, and would be happy to wait on her upstairs with any tidings that she might enquire for.

"By no means," she said, haughtily. She would wait for tidings rather than learn them from Lord Lovat. She turned, and went upstairs again, stung by hearing Lord Lovat's hateful laugh behind her as she went.

4

As she sat by the fire, devouring her shame and wrath, her attendant came up with a handful of newspapers, and Lord Lovat's compliments, and he had sent her the latest Edinburgh news to read, as she did not wish to hear it from him. She snatched the papers, meaning to thrust them into the fire in token of contempt for the sender; but a longing to read them came over her, and she might convey sufficient contempt by throwing them on the bed—and this she accordingly did.

She watched them, however, as a cat does a mouse. The woman seemed to have no intention of going down any more to-day. Whether the lady was watched, and her impatience detected, through the hole in the door, or whether humanity suggested that the unhappy creature should be permitted an hour of solitude on such an occasion, the woman was called down, and did not immediately return.

How impatiently, then, were the papers seized! How unsettled was the eye which ran over the columns, while the mind was too feverish to comprehend what it read! In a little while, however, the ordinary method of newspaper reading established itself, and she went on from one item to another with more amusement than anxiety. In this mood, and with the utmost suddenness, she came upon the announcement, in large letters, of "The Funeral of Lady Carse!" It was even so! In one paper was a paragraph intimating the threatening illness of Lady Carse; in the next, the announcement of her death; in the third, a full account of her funeral, as taking place from her husband's house.

Her fate was now clear. She was lost to the world for ever! In the midst of the agony of this doom she could yet be stung by the thought that this was the cause of Lord Lovat's complaisance in sending her the newspapers; that here was the reason of the only indulgence which had been permitted her!

As for the rest, her mind made short work of it. Her object must now be to confound her foes—to prove to the world that she was not dead and buried. From this place she could not do this. Here there was no scope and no hope. In travelling, and in her future residence, there might be a thousand opportunities. She could not stay here another hour, and so she sent word to Mr. Forster. His reply was that he should be happy to escort her that night. From the stair-head she told him that she could not wait till night. He declared it impossible to make provision for her comfort along the road without a few hours' notice by a horseman sent forward. The messenger was already saddling his horse, and by nine in the evening the rest of the party would follow.

At nine the lady was on her pillion, but now comfortably clad in a country dress—homely, but warm. It was dark, but she was informed that the party thoroughly knew their road, and that in four or five days they should have the benefit of the young moon.

So, after four or five days, they were to be still travelling ! Where could they be carrying her ?

# CHAPTER V.

## CROSS ROADS AND SHORT SEAS.

WHERE they were carrying her was more than Lady Carse herself could discover. To the day of her death she never knew what country she had traversed during the dreary and fatiguing week which ensued. She saw Stirling Castle standing up on its mighty rock against the dim sky; and she knew that before dawn they had entered the Highlands. But beyond this she was wholly ignorant. In those days there were no milestones on the road she travelled. The party went near no town, stopped at no inn, and never permitted her an opportunity of speaking to anyone out of their own number. They always halted before daylight at some solitary house — left open for them, but uninhabited — or at some cowshed, where they shook down straw for her bed, made a fire, and cooked their food; and at night they always remounted, and rode for many hours, through a wild country, where the most hopeful of captives could not dream of rescue. Sometimes they carried torches while ascending a narrow ravine, where a winter torrent dashed down the steep rocks and whirled away below, and where the lady unawares showed her desire to live by clinging faster to the horseman behind whom she rode. Sometimes she saw the whole starry hemi-

sphere resting like a dome on a vast moorland, the stars
rising from the horizon here and sinking there, as at sea.
The party rarely passed any farmsteads or other dwellings;
and when they did silence was commanded, and the riders
turned their horses on the grass or soft earth, in order to
appear as little as possible like a cavalcade to any wakeful
ears.    Once, on such an occasion, Lady Carse screamed
aloud; but this only caused her to be carried at a gallop,
which instantly silenced her, and then to be gagged for the
rest of the night.    She would have promised to make no
such attempt again, such a horror had she now of the muffle
which bandaged her mouth, but nobody asked her to
promise.    On the contrary, she heard one man say to
another, that the lady might scream all night long now, if
she liked; nobody but the eagles would answer her, now
she was among the Frasers.

Among the Frasers!    Then she was on Lord Lovat's
estates.    Here there was no hope for her; and all her
anxiety was to get on, though every step removed her
further from her friends, and from the protection of law.
But this was exactly the place where she was to stop for a
considerable time.

Having arrived at a solitary house among moorland hills,
Mr. Forster told her that she would live here till the days
should be longer, and the weather warm enough for a more
comfortable prosecution of her further journey.    He would
advise her to take exercise in the garden, small as it was,

and to be cheerful, and preserve her health, in expectation of the summer, when she would reach a place where all restrictions on her personal liberty would cease. He would now bid her farewell.

"You are going back to Edinburgh," said she, rising from her seat by the fire. "You will see Lord Carse. Tell him that though he has buried his wife, he has not got rid of her. She will haunt him—she will shame him—she will ruin him yet."

"I see now——" observed a voice behind her. She turned and perceived Lord Lovat, who addressed himself to Mr. Forster, saying,

"I see now that it *is* best to let such people live. If she were dead, we cannot say but that she might haunt him ; though I myself have no great belief of it. As it is, she is safe out of his way—at any rate, till she dies first. I see now that his method is the right one."

"Why, I don't know, my lord," replied Lady Carse. "You should consider how little trouble it would have cost to put me out of the way in my grave; and how much trouble I am costing you now. It is some comfort to me to think of the annoyance and risk, and fatigue and expense, I am causing you all."

"You mistake the thing, madam. We rejoice in these things, as incurred for the sake of some people over the water. It gratifies our loyalty—our loyalty, madam, is a sentiment which exalts and endears the meanest services, even that of sequestrating a spy, an informer."

"Come, come, Lovat, it is time we were off," said Mr. Forster, who was at once ashamed of his companion's brutality, and alarmed at its effect upon the lady. She looked as if she would die on the spot. She had not been aware till now how her pride had been gratified by the sense of her own importance, caused by so many gentlemen of consequence entering into her husband's plot against her liberty. She was now rudely told that it was all for their own sakes. She was controlled not as a dignified and powerful person, but as a mischievous informer. She rallied quickly—not only through pride, but from the thought that power is power, whencesoever derived, and that she might yet make Lord Lovat feel this. She curtseyed to the gentlemen, saying,

"It is your turn now to jeer, gentlemen; and to board up windows, and the like. The day may come when I shall sit at a window to see your heads fall."

"Time will show," said Lord Lovat, with a smile, and an elegant bow. And they left her alone.

They no longer feared to leave her alone. Her temper was well known to them; and her purposes of ultimate revenge, once clearly announced, were a guarantee that she would, if possible, live to execute them. She would make no attempts upon her life henceforward.

Weeks and months passed on. The snow came, and lay long, and melted away. Beyond the garden wall she saw sprinklings of young grass among the dark heather; and now the bleat of a lamb, and now the scudding brood of the moor-fowl, told her that spring was come. Long lines of wild geese in the upper air, winging steadily northwards, indicated the advancing season. The whins within view

SHE CURTSEYED TO THE GENTLEMEN.

burst into blossom; and the morning breeze which dried the dews wafted their fragrance. Then the brooding mists drew off under the increasing warmth of the sun; and the lady discovered that there was a lake within view—a wide expanse, winding away among mountains till it was lost behind their promontories. She strained her eyes to see vessels on this lake, and now and then she did perceive a little sail hoisted, or a black speck, which must be a row-boat traversing the waters when they were sheeny in the declining sun. These things, and the lengthening and warmth of the days, quickened her impatience to be removed. She often asked the people of the house whether no news and no messengers had come; but they did not improve in their knowledge of the English tongue any more than she did in that of the Gaelic, and she could obtain no satisfaction. In the sunny mornings she lay on the little turf-plat in the garden, or walked restlessly among the cabbage-beds (being allowed to go no further), or shook the locked gate desperately, till someone came out to warn her to let it alone. In the June nights she stood at her window, only one small pane of which would open, watching the mists shifting and curling in the moonlight, or the sheet lightning which now and then revealed the lake in the bosom of the mountains, or appeared to lay open the whole sky. But June passed away, and there was no change. July came and went—the sun was visibly shortening his daily journey, and leaving an hour of actual darkness in the middle of the night : and still there was no prospect of a further journey. She began to doubt Mr. Forster as much as she hated Lord Lovat, and to say to herself that his promises of further personal liberty in the summer were mere coaxing words, uttered to secure a quiet retreat from her presence. If she could see him, for only five minutes, how she would tell him her mind!

She never again saw Mr. Forster: but, one night in August, while she was at the window, and just growing sleepy, she was summoned by the woman of the house to dress herself for a night ride. She prepared herself eagerly enough, and was off presently, without knowing anything of the horsemen who escorted her.

It was with a gleam of pleasure that she saw that they were approaching the lake she had so often gazed at from afar: and her heart grew lighter still when she found that she was to traverse it. She began to talk, in her new exhilaration; and she did not leave off, though nobody replied. But her exclamations about the sunrise, the clearness of the water, and the leaping of the fish, died away when she looked from face to face of those about her, and found them all strange and very stern. At last, the dip of the oars was the only sound; but it was a pleasant and soothing one. All went well this day. After landing, the party proceeded westwards—as they did nightly for nearly a week. It mattered little that they did not enter a house in all that time. The weather was so fine, that a sheepfold, or a grassy nook of the moorland, served all needful purposes of a resting place by day.

On the sixth night, a surprise, and a terrible surprise, awaited the poor lady. Her heart misgave her when the night wind brought the sound of the sea to her ears—the surging sea which tosses and roars in the rocky inlets of the western coast of Scotland. But her dismay was dreadful when she discovered that there was a vessel below, on board which she was to be carried without delay. On the instant, dreadful visions arose before her imagination, of her being carried to a foreign shore, to be delivered into the hands of the Stuarts, to be punished as a traitor and spy ; and of those far off plantations and dismal colonies where people troublesome to their families were said to be sent, to be chained to servile labour with criminals and slaves. She wept bitterly : she clasped her hands—she threw herself at the feet of the conductor of the party—she appealed to them all, telling them to do what they would with her, if only they would not carry her to sea. Most of them looked at one another, and made no reply—not understanding her language. The conductor told her to fear nothing, as she was in the hands of the Macdonalds, who had orders from Sir Alexander Macdonald, of Skye, to provide for her safety. He promised that the voyage would not be a long one ; and that as soon as the sloop should have left the loch she should be told where she was going. With that, he lifted her lightly, stepped into a boat, and was rowed to the sloop, where she was received by the owner, and half a dozen other Macdonalds. For some hours they waited for a wind ; and sorely did the master wish it would come ; for the lady lost not a glimpse of an opportunity of pleading her cause, explaining that she was stolen from Edinburgh, against the laws. He told her she had better be quiet, as nothing could be done. Sir Alexander Macdonald was in the affair. He, for one, would never keep her or anyone against their will,

WATCHING THE VANISHING OF THE LAND.

unless Sir Alexander Macdonald were in it : but nothing could be done. He saw, however, that some impression was made on one person, who visited the sloop on business, one William Tolney, who had connexions at Inverness, from having once been a merchant there, and who was now a tenant of the Macleods, in a neighbouring island. This man was evidently touched ; and the Macdonalds held a consultation in consequence, the result of which was that William Tolney was induced to be silent on what he had seen and heard. But for many a weary year after did Lady Carse turn with hope to the image of the stranger who had listened to her on board the sloop, taken the address of her lawyer, and said that in his opinion something must be done.

In the evening the wind rose, and the sloop moved down the loch. With a heavy heart the lady next morning watched the vanishing of the last of Glengarry's seats, on a green platform between the grey and bald mountains ; then the last fishing hamlet on the shores ; and, finally, a flock of herons come abroad to the remotest point of the shore from their roosting places in the tall trees that sheltered Glengarry's abode. After that all was wretchedness. For many days she was on the tossing sea—the sloop now scudding before the wind, now heaving on the troubled waters, now creeping along between desolate looking islands, now apparently lost amidst the boundless ocean. At length, soon after sunrise, one bright morning, the sail was taken in, and the vessel lay before the entrance of an harbour which looked like the mouth of a small river. At noon the sun beat hot on the deck of the sloop. In the afternoon the lady impatiently asked what they were waiting for—if this really was, as she was told, their place of destination. The wind was not contrary; what where they waiting for?

"No, madam; the wind is fair. But it is a curious circumstance about this harbour that it can be entered safely only at night. It is one of the most dangerous harbours in all the isles."

"And you dare to enter it at night? What do you mean?"

"I will show you, madam, when night comes."

Lady Carse suspected that the delay was on her account; that she was not to land by daylight, less too much sympathy should be excited by her among the inhabitants. Her indignation at this stimulated her to observe all she could of the appearance of the island, in case of opportunity occurring to turn to the account of an escape any knowledge she might obtain. On the rocky ledges which stretched out into the sea lay basking several seals; and all about them, and on every higher ledge, were myriads of puffins. Hundreds of puffins and fulmars were in the air, and skimming the waters. The fulmars poised themselves on their long wings; the fat little puffins poffled about in the water, and made a great commotion were everything else was quiet. From these lower ridges of rock vast masses arose, black and solemn, some perpendicular, some with a slope too steep and smooth to permit a moment's dream of climbing them. Even on this warm day of August the clouds had not risen above the highest peaks; and they threw a

gloom over the interior of the small island, while the
skirting rocks and sea were glittering in the sunshine.
Even the scanty herbage of the slopes at the top of the
rocks looked almost a bright green where the sun fell
upon it; and especially where it descended so far as to
come into contrast with the blackness of the yawning
caverns with which the rocky wall was here and there
perforated.

The lady perceived no dwellings; but Macdonald, who
observed her searching gaze, pointed his glass and invited
her to look through it. At first she saw nothing but
a dim confusion of grey rocks and dull grass; but at length
she made out a grey cottage, with a roof of turf, and a peat
stack beside it.

" I see one dwelling," said the lady.

"You see it," observed Macdonald, satisfied, and re-
suming his glass. Then, observing the lady was not
satisfied, he added, " There are more dwellings, but
they are behind yonder ridge, out of sight. That is
where my place is."

Lady Carse did not at present discern where the dangerous
sympathy with her case was to come from. But there was
no saying how many dwellings there might be behind that
ridge. She once more insisted on landing by daylight;
and was once more told that it was out of the question.
She resolved to keep as wide awake as her suspicions, in
order to see what was to be done with her. She was

anxiously on the watch in the darkness an hour before midnight, when Macdonald said to her,

"Now for it, madam! I will presently show you something curious."

The sloop began to move under the soft breathing night
wind; and in a few minutes Macdonald asked her if she
saw anything before her, a little to the right. At first she
did not; but was presently told that a tiny spark, too
minute to be noticed by any but those who were looking
for it, was a guiding light.

"Where is it?" asked the lady. "Why have not you a
more effectual light?"

"We are thankful enough to have any: and it serves our
turn."

"Oh! I suppose it is a smuggler's signal, and it would
not do to make it more conspicuous."

"No, madam. It is far from being a smuggler's signal.
There is a woman, Annie Fleming, living in the grey house
I showed you, an honest and pious soul, who keeps up that
light for all that want it."

"Why? Who employs her?"

"She does it of her own liking. Some have heard tell,
but I don't know it for true, that when she and her husband
were young she saw him drown, from his boat having run
foul in the harbour that she overlooks, and that from that
day to this she has had a light up there every night. I can
say that I never miss it when I come home; and I always

5

enter by night, trusting to it as the best landmark in this diflicult harbour."

"And do the other inhabitants trust to it, and come in by night ? "

Macdonald answered that his was the only boat on the island; but he believed that all who had business on the sea between this and Skye knew that light, and made use of it, on occasion, in dangerous weather. And now he must not talk, but see to his vessel.

This is the only boat on the island ! He must mean the only sloop. There must be fishing boats. There must and should be, the lady resolved; for she would get back to the mainland. She would not spend her days here, beyond the westerly Skye, where she had just learned that this island lay.

The anxious business of entering the harbour was accomplished by slow degrees, under the guidance of the spark on the hill side. At dawn the little vessel was moored to a natural pier of rock, and the lady was asked whether she would proceed to Macdonald's house immediately or take some hours' rest first.

Here ended her fears of being secluded from popular sympathy. She was weary of the sea and the vessel, and made all haste to leave them.

Her choice lay between walking and being carried by Highlanders. She chose to walk; and with some fatigue, and no little internal indignation, she traversed a mile and a half of rocky and moorland ways, then arriving at a sordid and dreary looking farmhouse, standing alone in a wild place, to which Macdonald proudly introduced her as Sir Alexander's estate on this island, of which he was the tenant.

# CHAPTER VI.

## THE STEADFAST.

It was a serene evening when, the day after her landing, Lady Carse approached Widow Fleming's abode. The sun was going down in a clear sky; and when, turning from the dazzling western sea, the eye wandered eastwards, the view was such as could not but transport a heart at ease. The tide was low, and long shadows from the rocks lay upon the yellow sands and darkened, near the shore, the translucent sea. At the entrance of the black caverns the spray leaped up on the advance of every wave,—not in threatening but as if at play. Far away over the lilac and green waters arose the craggy peaks of Skye, their projections and hollows in the softest light and shadow. As the sea birds rose from their rest upon the billows, opposite the sun, diamond drops fell from their wings. Nearer at hand there was little beauty but what a brilliant sunset sheds over every scene. There were shadows from the cottage over the dull green sward, and from the two or three goats which moved about on the ledges and slopes of the upper rocks. The cottage itself was more lowly and much more odd than the lady had conceived from anything she had yet seen or heard of. Its walls were six feet thick, and roofed from the inside, leaving a sort of platform all round, which

60

was overgrown with coarse herbage. The outer and inner surfaces of the wall were of stones, and the middle part was filled in with earth; so that grass might well grow on the top. The roof was of thatch—part straw, part sods, tied down to cross poles by ropes of twisted heather. The walls did not rise more than five feet from the ground; and nothing could be easier than for the goats to leap up, when tempted to graze there. A kid was now amusing itself on one corner. As Lady Carse walked round, she was startled at seeing a woman sitting on the opposite corner. Her back was to the sun—her gaze fixed on the sea, and her fingers were busy knitting. The lady had some doubts at first about its being the widow, as this woman wore a bright cotton handkerchief tied over her head: but a glance at the face when it was turned towards her assured her that it was Annie Fleming herself.

"No, do not come down," said the lady. "Let me come up beside you. I see the way."

And she stepped up by means of the projecting stones of the wall, and threw herself down beside the quiet knitter.

"What are you making? Mittens? And what of? What sort of wool is this?"

"It is goats' hair."

"Tiresome work!" the lady observed. "Wool is bad enough; but these short lengths of hair! I should never have patience."

The widow replied that she had time in these summer

evenings; and she was glad to take the chance of selling a few pairs when Macdonald went to the main, once or twice a year.

"How do they sell? What do you get for them?"

SHE THREW HERSELF DOWN BESIDE THE QUIET KNITTER.

"I get oil to last me for some time."

"And what else?"

"Now and then I may want something else; but I get chiefly oil—as what I want most."

The widow saw that Lady Carse was not attending to what she said, and was merely making an opening for what she herself wanted to utter: so Annie said no more of her work and its payment, but waited.

"This is a dreadful place," the lady burst out. "Nobody can live here."

"I have heard there are kindlier places to live in," the widow replied. "This island must appear rather bare to people who come from the south,—as I partly remember myself."

"Where did you come from? Do you know where I come from? Do you know who I am?" cried the lady.

"I came from Dumfries. I have not heard where you lived, my lady. I was told by Macdonald that you came by Sir Alexander Macdonald's orders, to live here henceforward."

"I will not live here henceforward. I would sooner die."

The widow looked surprised. In answer to that look Lady Carse said,

"Ah! you do not know who I am, nor what brought me here, or you would see that I cannot live here, and why I would rather die.—Why do not you speak? Why do you not ask me what I have suffered?"

"I should not think of it, my lady. Those who have suffered are slow to speak of their heart pain, and would be ashamed before God to say how much oftener they would rather have died."

"I must speak, however, and I will," declared Lady
Carse. "You know I must; and you are the only person
in the island that I can speak to.—I want to live with you.
I must. I know you are a good woman. I know you are
kind. If you are kind to mere strangers that come in
boats, and keep a light to save them from shipwreck, you
will not be cruel to me—the most ill used creature—the
most wretched—the most——"

She hid her face on her knees, and wept bitterly.

"Take courage, my lady," said Annie. "If you have not
strength enough for your troubles to-day, it only shows that
there is more to come."

"I do not want strength," said the lady. "You do not
know me. I am not wanting in strength. What I want—
what I must have—is justice."

"Well—that is what we are all most sure of when God's
day comes," said Annie. "That we are quite sure of. And
we may surely hope for patience till then, if we really wish
it. So I trust you will be comforted, my lady."

"I cannot stay here, however. There are no people
here. There is nobody that I can endure at Macdonald's,
and there are none others but labourers, and they speak only
Gaelic. And it is a wretched place. They have not even
bread.—Mrs. Fleming, I must come and live with you."

"I have no bread, my lady. I have nothing so good as
they have at Macdonald's."

"You have a kind heart. Never mind the bread now.

We will see about that. I don't care how I live; but I want to stay with you. I want never to go back to Macdonald's."

The widow stepped down to the ground, and beckoned to the lady to follow her into the house. It was a poor place as could be seen :—one room with a glazed window looking towards the harbour, a fireplace and a bed opposite the window ;—a rickety old bedstead, with an exhausted flock bed and a rug upon it; and from one end of the apartment, a small dim space partitioned off, in which was a still less comfortable bed, laid on trestles made of drift-wood.

"Who sleeps here?"

"My son, when he is at home. He is absent now, my lady: and see, this is the only place ;—no place for you, my lady."

Lady Carse shrank back impatiently. She then turned and said,

"I might have this larger room, and you the other. I shall find means of paying you——"

"Impossible, madam," the widow replied. "I am obliged to occupy this room."

"For to-night, at least, you will let me have it. I cannot go back to Macdonald's to-night. I will not go back at all; and you cannot turn me out to-night. I have other reasons besides those I mentioned. I must be in sight of the harbour. It is my only hope."

"You can stay here, if you will, madam : and you can have that bed.   But I can never leave this room between dark and light.   I have yonder lamp to attend to."

"Oh! I will attend to the lamp."

The widow smiled, and observed that she hoped the lady would have better sleep than she could enjoy if she had the lamp to watch; and that was a business which she could not commit to another hand.   In the course of the argument, the lady discovered that it would be a serious matter to let out both the fire and lamp, as there was no tinder-box on the island, and no wood, except in the season of storms, when some was drifted up wet.

"I should like to live with you, and help you to keep up your lamp," said the lady.   "If you could only manage a room for me——Not that I mean to stay in this island! I will not submit to that.   But while I am waiting to get away, I should like to spend my time with you.   You have a heart.   You would feel for me."

"I do feel for you, madam.   This must be a terrible place for you, just to-day,—and for many days to come. But oh! my lady, if you want peace of mind, this is the place!   It is a blessing that may be had anywhere, I know. One would think it shone down from the sky or breathed out from the air,—it is so sure to be wherever the sky bends over, or the air wraps us round.   But of all places, this is the one for peace of mind."

"This !—this dreary island !"

"This quiet island. Look out now, and see if you can call it dreary. Why, madam, there can hardly be a brighter glory, or a more cheerful glow among the sons of God about the throne, than there is at this moment over sea and shore, and near at home up to the very stone of my threshold. Madam, I could never think this island dreary."

"It is not always sunset, nor always summer time," said Lady Carse, who could not deny nor wholly resist the beauty of the scene.

"Other beauty comes by night and in the winter," observed the widow, "and at times a grandeur which is better than the beauty. If the softness of this sunshine nourishes our peace of mind, yet more does the might of the storms. The beauty might be God's messenger. The might is God Himself."

"You speak as if you did not fear God," said the lady, with the light inexperience of one to whom such subjects were not familiar.

"As a sinner, I fear Him, madam. But as His child—— Why, madam, what else have we in all the universe? And having Him, what more do we want?"

"He has made us full of wants," said the lady. "I, for one, am all bereaved, and very, very wretched.—But do not let us talk of that now. One who is alone in this place, and knows and needs nothing beyond, cannot enter into my sorrows at once. It will take long to make you conceive such misery as mine. But it will be a comfort to me to open my heart to you. And I must live within view of the harbour. I must see every boat that comes. They say you do."

"I do. They are few; but I see them all."

"And you save a good many by the spark in your window."

"It has pleased God to save some, it is thought, who would have perished as some perished before them. He set me that task, in a solemn way, many years ago; and any mercy that has grown out of it is His.—Do you see any vessel on the sea, madam? I always look abroad the last thing before the sun goes down. My eyes can hardly be much older than yours; but they are much worn."

"How have you so used your eyes? Is it that hair-knitting?"

"That is not good. But it is more the sharp winds, and the night watching, and the shine of the sea in the day."

"I must live with you. I will watch for you, night and day. You think I cannot. You think I shall tire. Why, you are not weary of it."

"Oh, no! I shall never be weary of it."

"Much less should I. You want only to keep up your lamp. I want to get away. All the interests of my life lie beyond this sea; and do you think I shall tire of watching for the opportunity?—I will watch through this very night. You shall go to bed, and sleep securely, and I will keep your lamp. And to-morrow we will arrange something.

Why should I not have a room,—a cottage built at the end of yours? I will."

"If you could find anyone to build it," suggested the widow.

"Somebody built Macdonald's, I suppose. And yours."

"Macdonald's is very old;—built, it is thought, at the same time with the chapel, which has been in ruins these hundred years. My husband built ours,—with me to help him; and also his brother, who died before it was finished."

"Where is your son?" inquired the lady. "If he will undertake to work for me, I will get it done. Where is your son? And what is his business?"

"I do not know exactly where he is."

"Well, but is he on the island?"

"I believe so. He comes and goes according to his business. In the early summer he seeks eggs all over the island; and, somewhat later, the eider-down. When he can get nothing better he brings the birds themselves."

"What do you do with them?"

"We keep the feathers, and also the skins. The skins are warm to cover the feet with, when made into socks. If the birds are not very old, we salt them for winter food: and at worst, I get some oil from them. But I get most oil from the young seals, and from the livers of the fish he catches at times."

"Fish! then he has a boat! Does he go out in a boat to fish?"

"I can hardly say that he has a boat," replied the mother, with an extraordinary calmness of manner that told of internal effort. "Our caverns run very deep into the rocks; and the ledges run out far into the sea. Rollo has made a kind of raft of the drift-wood he found: and on this he crosses the water in the caverns, and passes from ledge to ledge, fishing as he goes. This is our only way of getting fish, except when a chance boat comes into the harbour."

"Could that raft go out on a calm day,—on a very smooth sea,—to meet any boat at a distance?"

"Impossible! madam. I think it too dangerous in our smallest coves to be used without sin. It is against my judgment that Rollo ever goes round the end of a ledge, which he has been seen to do."

"But it is impossible to get a boat? Have you never had a boat?"

"We once had a boat, madam: and it was lost."

Even the selfish Lady Carse reproached herself for her question. It struck her now that boat and husband had been lost together; for Macdonald had told her that Annie Fleming had seen her husband drown.

"I wish I knew where Rollo is," she said to break the silence. "I think something might be done. I think I could find a way. Do not you wish you knew where he was?"

"No, madam."

"Well! perhaps you might be uneasy about him if you did. But which way did he go?"

The widow pointed northwards, where huge masses of rock appeared tumbled one upon another, and into the sea, at the base of a precipice two hundred feet high. She further told, in reply to a question, that Rollo went forth yesterday, without saying where he was going ; and there were caves among the rocks she had pointed out, where Rollo might possibly be fishing.

Lady Carse found it vexatious that darkness was coming on. She had a purpose ; but the sun did not set the later, nor promise to rise the earlier, on that account. When the widow set before her some oaten bread and dried fish, she ate, without perceiving that none was left for her hostess. And when the widow lighted the iron lamp and set it in the window, the lady made only faint pretences of a wish to sit up and watch it. She also said nothing of occupying the meaner bed. She was persuaded that her first duty was to obtain some good rest, preparatory to going forth to seek Rollo, and induce him to take her on his raft to some place whence she might escape to the mainland. So she lay down on the widow's bed, and slept soundly, — her hungry hostess sitting by the smouldering peats in the rude fireplace, — now and then smiling at the idea of her guest's late zeal about watching the lamp for her, in order to give her a good night's rest. When daylight came, she retired to her son's bed, and had just dropped asleep when Lady Carse roused her to ask for some breakfast to take with her, as she did not know when she should be back from her expedition. Again the widow smiled as she said there was nothing in the house. At this time of the year there were no stores; and a good appetite at night left nothing for the morning.

"O dear!" said the lady. "Well: I daresay your sitting up made you hungry enough to finish everything while I was asleep. No doubt it must. But what to do I know not. I will not go back to Macdonald's, if I starve for it. Perhaps I may meet some fishermen, or somebody. I will try.—Good morning. I shall come back: but I will not put you long out of your ways. I will get a cottage built at the end of yours as soon as possible." The door closed behind her, and once more the widow smiled, as she composed herself to rest on her own bed. She had already returned thanks for the blessings with which the new day had opened; and especially that to one so lowly as herself was permitted the honour and privilege—so unlooked for and unthought of—of dispensing hospitality.

# CHAPTER VII.

### THE ROVING OF THE RESTLESS.

THE lady began walking at a great rate, being in a vast hurry to find Rollo. She descended to the shore, knowing that if she kept on the heights she should arrive at the precipices which would forbid all access to the caves below. The tide was going down; and as soon as she reached the sands of a little cove she was pleased to see a good many shell fish. Her first thought was that she would collect some and carry them up for Annie Fleming's breakfast; but she immediately remembered that this would add to her fatigues, and consume her precious time; and she gave up the thought, and began picking up cockles for herself—large blue cockles, which she thought would afford her an excellent breakfast, if only she could meet with some fresh bread and butter in some nook in the island. She turned up her skirt—the skirt of the country woman's gown which she wore—and made a bag of it for her cockles, rejoicing for the moment that it was not one of her own silks. Then she remembered that she had seen at the widow's a light and strong frail basket, made of the sea-bent which grew in the sands. This basket would be useful to her: so she would, after all, go up—carry some cockles for Annie, and

borrow the basket.  She did so, and came away again
without awakening the widow.

At first, Lady Carse thought that Annie was right, and
that the island was not so dreary after all.  The morning
breeze was fresh and strengthening ; the waves ran up gaily

BEGAN PICKING UP COCKLES.

upon the sands, and leaped against the projecting rocks,
and fell back with a merry splash.  And the precipices were
so fine, she longed for her sketch-book ; and the romance of
her youth began to revive within her.  Here was a whole
day for roving.  She would somehow make a fire in a cave,
and cook for herself.  She was sure she could live among

these caves; and if she was missing for a considerable time, the Macdonalds would think she had escaped, or was drowned; and she could slip away at last, when some vessel put into the harbour. She stopped and looked round; but on all the vast stretch of waters there was no vessel to be seen but the sloop in the harbour; while on shore there was no human being visible, nor any trace of habitation. The solitude rather pressed on her heart; but she hastened on, and rounded the point which would shut out from her the land view, and prevent her being seen by any one from Macdonald's. She had no fear of her return being cut off by the tide. She had the whole day before her, and could climb the rocks to a safe height at any time.

These were caves indeed! At sight of them her heart was in a sort of tumult very different from any it had experienced for long. She eagerly entered the first, and drew deep breath as the thunder of the waters and the echoes together almost confounded her senses. At the lowest tides there was some depth of water below, in a winding central channel. In the evening how black that channel must be! how solemn the whole place! Now the low sun was shining in, lighting up every point, and disclosing all the hollows, and just catching a ripple now and then, which, in its turn, made a ripple of light on the roof; and, far in, there was an opening—a gaping chink in the side of the cave—which gave admission to a second rocky chamber.

Lady Carse was bent on reaching this opening; and did

so, at last. She could not cross the clear deep water in the channel below her. It was just too wide for a safe leap. But she found a footing over the rocks which confined it; and on she went—now ascending, now descending almost to the water—amidst dancing lights and rising and falling echoes; on she went, her heart throbbing, her spirits cheered—her whole soul full of a joy which she had not experienced for long. She stepped over the little chasm to which the waters narrowed at last, and, reaching the opening thrust herself through it.

She seemed to have left light and sound behind her. Dim, cool, and almost silent was the cavern she now stood in. Its floor was thickly strewn with fine sand, conveying the sensation that her own footsteps were not to be heard. Black pillars of rock rose from a still pool which lay in her way, and which she perceived only just in time to prevent her stepping into it. These pillars and other dark masses of rock sprang up and up till her eye lost them in the darkness; and if there was a roof, she could not see it. A drip from above made a plash about once in a minute in the pool; and the murmur from without was so subdued—appeared to be so swallowed up in vastness and gloom—that the minute drop was loud in comparison. Lady Carse lay down on the soft sand, to rest, and listen, and think—to ponder plans of hiding and escape. All her meditations brought her round to the same point: that three things were necessary to any plan of escape—a supply of food, a boat, and an accomplice. She arose, chilled and hungry, determined to try whether she could not meet with one or all of these this very day.

As she slowly proceeded round the pool, she became aware that it was not so perfectly still as hitherto; and a gurgle of waters grew upon the car. It was only that the tide was coming up, and that the pool was being fed by such influx as could take place through a few crannies. She perceived that these crannies had let in a glimmering of light which was now sensibly darkened. She had no fear—only the delicious awe which thrills through the spirit on its admission to the extreme privacies of nature. There was some light, and safe opportunity of return by the way she had come. She would not go back till she had tried whether she could get on.

On she went—more than once in almost total darkness—more than once slipping on a piece of wet and weedy rock where she expected to tread on thick sand—more than once growing irritable at little difficulties, as hungry people of better tempers than hers are apt to do in strange places. A surprise awaited her at last. She had fancied she perceived a glimmer of light before her; and she suddenly found herself at the top of a steep bank of sand, at the bottom of which there was an opening—a very low arch—to the outer air. While she was sliding down this bank, she heard a voice outside. She was certain of it. Presently there was a laugh, and the voice again. If she had found

Rollo, there was somebody else too; and if Rollo was not here, there was the more to hope something from.

Now the question was whether she could get through the arch. She pushed her basket through first, and then her own head; and she saw what made her lie still for some little time. The arch opened upon a cove, deep and narrow, between projecting rocks. A small raft rose and fell on the surface of the water; and on the raft stood a man, steading himself with his legs wide apart, while he held a rope with both hands, and gazed intently upwards. The raft was in a manner anchored; tied with ropes to masses of rock on each side of the cove; but it still pitched so much that Lady Carse thought the situation of the man very perilous: and she, therefore, made no noise, lest she should startle him. She little dreamed how safe was his situation compared with that of the comrade he was watching.

In a short time the man changed his occupation. He relaxed his hold of the rope, fastened it to a corner of the raft, gazed about him like a man of leisure, and then once more looked upwards, holding out his arms as if to catch something good. And immediately a shower of sea-birds began to fall: now one, now three, now one again; down they came, head foremost, dead as a stone. Two fell into the water; but he fished them up with a stick with a noose of hair at the end, and flung them on the heap in the middle of the raft.

When the shower began to slacken, Lady Carse thought it the time to make herself heard. She put her head and shoulders through the low arch, and asked the man if he thought she could get through. His start at the voice, his bewildered look down the face of the rock, and the scared expression of his countenance when he discovered the face that peeped out at the bottom, amused Lady Carse extremely. She did not remember how unlike her fair complexion and her hair were to those of the women of these islands, nor that a stranger was in this place more rare than a ghost. And as for the man—what could he suppose but that the handsome face that he saw peeping out, laughing, from the base of the precipice, was that of some rock spirit, sent perhaps for mischief? However, in course of time the parties came to an explanation; that is, of all that the lady said, the man caught one word—Macdonald; and he saw that she had a basket of cockles, and knew the basket to be of island manufacture. Moreover he found, when he ventured to help her out, that her hand was of flesh and blood, though he had never before seen one so slender and white.

When she stood upright on the margin of the creek, what a scene it was! Clear as the undulating waters were, no bottom was visible. Their darkness and depth sent a chill through her frame. Overhead the projecting rocks nearly shut out the sky, while the little strip that remained was darkened by a cloud of fluttering and screaming sea birds. The cause of their commotion was pointed out to her. A

man, whom she could scarcely have distinguished but for
the red cap on his head, was on the face of the precipice;
now appearing still, now moving, she could not tell how, for
the rock appeared to her as smooth up there as the wall of
a house.  But it was not so—there were ledges; and on
one of these he stood, plundering the nests of the sea fowl,
which were screaming round his head.

"Rollo?" the lady asked, as she turned away, her brain
reeling at the sight she had seen.

"Rollo," replied the man, now entirely satisfied.  No
spirit would want to be told who anyone was.

And now Rollo was to descend.  His comrade again
stepped upon the raft, pushed out to the middle of the
channel, secured the raft, grasped the rope, and steadied
himself.  Lady Carse thought she could not look; but she
glanced up now and then, when there was a call from
above, or a question from below, or when there was a fling
of the rope or a pause in the proceedings.  When Rollo at
last slid down upon the raft, hauled it to shore, and jumped
on the rock beside her, he was as careless as a hedger
coming home to breakfast, while she was trembling in every
limb.

And Rollo was thinking more of his breakfast than of
the way he had earned it, or of the presence of a stranger.
He was a stout, and now hungry, lad of eighteen, to whom
any precipice was no more startling than a ladder is to a
builder.  And, as his mother had taught him to speak

English, and he had on that account been employed to communicate with such strangers as had now and then come to the island during Macdonald's absence, he was little embarrassed by the apparition of the lady. He was chiefly occupied with his pouchful of eggs, there being more than he had expected to find so late in the season. It was all very well, he said, for their provision to-day; but it was a sign that somebody knew this cove as well as themselves, and that it was no longer a property to himself and his comrade.

"How so?" inquired the lady. "How can you possibly tell by the eggs that anyone has been here?"

Rollo glanced at his comrade, in a sort of droll assurance that it could be no voice from the grave, no ghostly inhabitant of a cave, who could require to have such a matter explained. He then condescendingly told her that when the eggs of the eider-duck are taken she lays more; and this twice over, before giving up in despair. Of course, this puts off the season of hatching; and when, therefore, eggs are found fresh so late in the season, it is pretty plain that someone has been there to take those earlier laid. Rollo seemed pleased that the lady could comprehend this when it was explained to her. He gave her an encouraging nod, and began to scramble onward over the rocks, his companion being already some paces in advance of him. The lady followed with her basket as well as she could; but she soon found herself alone, and in not the most amiable mood at being thus neglected.  She had not yet learned that she was in a place where women are accustomed to shift for themselves, and precedence is not thought of, except by the fireside, with aged people or a minister of the Gospel in presence.

She smoothed her brow, however, when she regained sight of the young men.  They were on their knees in the entrance of a cavern, carefully managing a smouldering peat so as to obtain a fire.  It was ticklish work; for the peat had been left to itself rather too long; and chips and shavings were things never seen in these parts.  A wisp of dry grass, or a few fibres of heather, were made to serve instead; and it was not easy to create with these heat enough to kindle fresh peats.  At last, however, it was done; and eggs were poked in, here and there, to roast. The cockles must be roasted, too; and two or three little mouse-coloured birds, the young of the eider-duck, were broiled as soon as plucked.  So much for the eating.  As for the drinking, there was nothing but pure whisky, unless the lady could drink sea-water.  Thirsty as she was she thought of the drip in the cave; but, besides that it was far to go, and scanty when obtained, she remembered all the slime she had seen, and she did not know whence that drip came.  So she gulped down two or three mouthfuls of whisky, and was surprised to find how little she disliked it, and how well it agreed with her after her walk.

As soon as Rollo could attend to her, she told him where

she had spent the night—how she had resolved to live with his mother, and in sight of the harbour—and how she wanted two or more rooms built for her at the end of the widow's cottage, unless, indeed, she could get a boat built instead, to take her over to the main, for which she would engage to pay hereafter whatever should be asked. Rollo told his companion this; and they both laughed so at the idea of the boat, that the lady rose in great anger, and walked away. Rollo attended her, and pointed to his raft' saying that there was no other such craft as even that in the island; and people did not think of boats, even in their dreams, though he could fancy that any lady in the south might, for he had heard that boats were common in the south. But, he went on to say, if she could not have a boat, she might have a house.

"Will you help to build it?" asked the lady. "Will your companion—will all the people you know—help me to build it?"

"Why, yes," Rollo replied. "We shall have to build some sort of a cottage for the minister that is coming—for the minister and his wife; and we may as well——"

"Minister! Is there a minister coming?" cried the lady. "O thank God, whose servant he is! Thank God for sending me deliverance, as He surely will by these means!"

She had sunk on her knees. Rollo patted her on the shoulder and said the folk were certainly coming.

What to make of Rollo she did not know. He treated

her as if she were a child. He used a coaxing way of talking, explained to her the plainest things before her eyes, and patted her on the shoulder. She drew away, looking very haughtily at him, but he only nodded.

"Why was I not told before that the minister and his wife were coming? Macdonald did not tell me. Your mother did not tell me."

"They do not know it yet. They seldom know things till I tell them; and I did not want to be kept at home to build a house till I had got some business of my own done."

He would not tell how he had obtained his information; but explained that it was the custom for a minister to live for some time on each of the outlying islands, where there were too few people to retain a constant pastor. This island was too little inhabited to have had a minister on its shores since the chapel had gone to ruin, a hundred years before—but the time was at hand at last. There had been a disappointment in some arrangements in the nearest neighbour islet; and Mr. Ruthven and his wife were appointed to reside here for a year or more, as might appear desirable. Rollo considered this great news. Children and betrothed persons would be brought hither to be baptized and married—arriving perhaps more than once in the course of the year; and it would be strange if the minister were not, in that time, to be sent for in a boat to bury somebody. Or, perhaps, a funeral or two might come to the old chapel. Some traffic there must be; and that would make it a great year for Rollo. And, to begin with, there would be the house to build; and he might be sent for materials. He should like that, though he did not much fancy the trouble of the building.

After a moment's thought the lady asked him if he could not keep the secret of the minister's coming till the last possible hour. She would reward him well if he would get the house built as for her. Seeing how precious was the opportunity, she gave Rollo her confidence, showed him how it would tend to satisfy Macdonald if she appeared to be settling herself quietly in the island; whereas, if he knew of the approach of vessels with strangers, he would probably imprison her, or carry her away to some yet wilder and more remote speck in the ocean.. Rollo saw something of her reasons, and said patronizingly,

"Why, you talk like an island woman now. You might almost have lived here, by the way you understand things."

Yet better did he apprehend her promises of vast rewards, if he would do exactly as she wished. There was an air about her which enabled him to fancy her some queen or other powerful personage; and as it happened to suit him to keep the secret till the last moment, he promised, for himself and his comrade, to be discreet, and obey orders.

This settled, the lady turned homewards, with a basket full of eggs, and fish, and young birds, and news for the widow that her son was safe, and not far off, and about to come home to try his hand at building a house.

# CHAPTER VIII.

## THE WAITING OF THE WISE.

THE house proceeded well. Macdonald had no express orders about it; but he had express orders to keep Lady Carse on the island, and, if possible, in a quiet and orderly state of manners. When he saw how completely engrossed she was in the building of this dwelling, and what a close friendship she appeared to have formed with Annie Fleming, he believed that she was a woman of a giddy mind and strong self-will, who might be managed by humouring. If he could assist her in providing herself with a succession of new objects, he hoped that she might be kept from mischief and misery, as a child is by a change of toys. He would try this method, and trust to his chief's repaying him any expenses incurred for the strange lady's sake. So he granted the use of his ponies and his people,—now a man or two,—and now their wives, to bring stones and earth and turf, and to twist heather bands. Once or twice he came himself, and lent a strong hand to raise a corner-stone, and help to lay the hearthstone. The house consisted of two rooms, divided by a passage. If Lady Carse had chosen to admit the idea of remaining after the arrival of the Ruthvens, she would have added a third room; but she had resolved that she would leave the island in the vessel which brought them, or in the next that their arrival would bring: and she would not dwell for an instant on any doubt of accomplishing her purpose.

So the thick walls rose, and the low roof was on, and the thatch well bound down, and secured moreover with heavy stones, before the autumn storms arrived. And before the hard rains came down, all Macdonald's ponies were one evening seen approaching in a string, laden with peat—a present to the lady. In the course of the day there was stacked, at the end of her cottage, enough to last for some months. When the widow came out to see it and wish her joy—for a good stack of well dried peat was the richest of all possessions in that region—the lady smiled as cheerfully as Annie; not at the peat, however, but at the thought that she should see little or none of it burn. She intended to dispose of her winter evenings far otherwise.

As for the widow, she was thankful now that she had never thought her situation dreary. If, in her former solitude, when her boy was absent, she had murmured at that solitude, her present feelings would have been a rebuke to her. She was not happy now; so far from it, that her former life appeared, in comparison with it, as happy as she could desire. Perhaps it had been too peaceful, she thought, and she might need some exercise of patience. It was a great advantage, certainly, for both herself and Rollo to hear the things the lady could tell of ways of living in other places, and to learn such a variety of knowledge from a person so much better informed than themselves. But then this knowledge appeared to be all so unsanctified! It did not make the poor lady herself strong in heart and peaceful in spirit. It was wonderful, and very stirring to the mind, to learn how wise people were who lived in cities, and what great ability was required to conduct the affairs of life where men were gathered together in numbers; but then these wonders did not seem to impress those who lived in the midst of them. There was no sign that they were watching and praising God's hand working among the faculties of men, as more retired people do in much meaner things—in the warmth which the eider duck gives to her eggs by wrapping them in down from her own breast, and the punctuality with which the herring shoals pass by in May and October, making the sea glitter with life and light as they go. She feared that when people lived out of sight of green pastures and still waters—and she looked at the moment upon the down on which the goats were browsing, and the fresh water pool, where the dragon fly hovered for a few hot days in summer—when men lived out of sight of green pastures and still waters, she feared that they became perplexed in a sort of Babel, where the call of the shepherd was too gentle to be heard. At least, it appeared thus from the effect upon Rollo of the lady's conversation. She had always feared for him the effect of seeing the world, as she remembered the world—of his seeing it before he had better learned to see God everywhere, and to be humble accordingly—and the conversation he now heard was to him much like being on the mainland, and even in a town. It had not made him more humble, or more kind, or more helpful; except, indeed, to the lady—there was nothing he would not do to help her.

And here Annie sighed and smiled at once, as the thought struck her that while she was mourning over other people's corruption she was herself not untouched. She detected herself admitting some dislike to the lady because she so occupied Rollo that he had left off supplying his mother with fishes' livers and seal-fat for oil. The best season had passed :—she had spoken to him several times not to lose the six-weeks-old seals ; but he had not attended to it ; and now her stock of oil was very low ; and the long winter nights were before her. She must speak to Macdonald to procure her some oil. But very strictly must she speak to herself about this new trouble of discontent. Did she not know that He who appointed her dwelling-place on that height, and who marked her for her life's task by that touch on her heart-strings the night she saw her husband drown, would supply the means? If her light was to be set on the hill for men to see from the tossing billows and be saved, it would be taken care of that, as of old, the widow's cruise of oil did not fail. What *she* had to look to was that the lamp of her soul did not grow dim and go out. How lately was she thanking God for the new opportunities afforded her by the arrival of this stranger! and now she was

7

shrinking from these very opportunities, and finding fault with everybody before herself!

There was some little truth in this, and it was very natural; for this kind of trial was new to Annie. But she never yielded to it again—not even when the trial was such as few would have been able to bear.

As the dark blustering month of November advanced, the widow's rheumatism came on more severely than ever before. She had given up her bed to Lady Carse, and when Rollo was at home, slept on the floor, on some ashes covered with a blanket; the only materials for a bed which she had been able to command, as Rollo had been too busy to get seal-skins, or go to any distance for heather while it was soft. She had caught cold repeatedly, and was likely to have a bad winter with her rheumatism, however soon the lady might get into her own house and yield up the widow's bed. One gusty afternoon, when the wet fogs were driving past, Annie waited long for the lady and Rollo to come in to the evening meal. She could not think what detained them next door in such weather; for it was no weather for working—besides that, it was getting dark. She could not, with her stiff and painful limbs, go out of doors; and when she perceived that her smallest lamp was gone, she satisfied herself that they had some particular work to finish for which they needed light, and would come in when it was done.

But it grew dark, and the wind continued to rise, and

they did not appear. They did not mean to appear this night. Macdonald had been informed, at last, from his chief, of the intended arrival of the minister and his lady; had been very angry at the long concealment of the news,

SITTING AT SUPPER OVER A GOOD FIRE.

and would now, Lady Carse apprehended, keep a careful watch over her, and probably confine her till the expected boats had come and gone. So she and her accomplices at once repaired to the cave—a cave which Rollo was sure

7—2

none of Macdonald's people had discovered—where for some time past Rollo and his comrade had stored dried fish, such small parcels of oatmeal as they could obtain, and plenty of peat for fuel. There they were now sitting at supper over a good fire, kindled in a deep sand, which would afford a warm and soft bed—they were at supper while the widow was waiting for them in pain and anxiety—and, at last, in cold and dreariness.

When the fire was low, she rose painfully from her seat, to feed it, and to trim and light the lamp. Alas! there were no peats in the corner. She knew there were plenty at mid-day: but Lady Carse had, at the last moment, bethought herself that the fuel in the cave might be damp, and had carried off those in the corner, desiring Rollo to bring in more from the stack to dry ; and this Rollo had neglected to do. The fire would be quite out in an hour. Annie saw that she must attempt to get out to the stack. She did attempt it; but the stormy blast and the thick cold drizzle so drove against her that she could not stand it, and could only with difficulty shut the door. She turned to her lamp, to light it while the fire was yet alive. There was but little oil in it. She reached out her hand for the oil can. It was not there. Rollo had considered that the lady would want light in the cave ; Lady Carse had considered that the widow might for one night make a good fire serve her purposes ; and so the oil can was gone to the same place with the peats.

Annie sank down on her seat, almost subdued. Not

quite subdued, however, even by this threat of the baffling of the great object of her life. Not quite subdued, for her heart and her ear were yet open to the voices of nature.

SHE LIGHTED THE LAMP WITH DIFFICULTY.

The scream of a sea-bird reached her, as the creature was swept by on the blast.

"That is for me," she said to herself, the blood returning to her stricken heart and pale cheek. "How God sends His creatures to teach us at the moment when we need His voice! I have seen the cormorant sitting in his hole in wintry weather,—sitting there for days together, hungry and cold, trying now and then to get out, and driven back by such a blast as he cannot meet,—by such a blast as this. And then he sits on patiently, and moves no more till the wind lulls and the sky clears. And if his wing is weak at first it soon strengthens. The blast drives me back to. night; but I, who have thoughts to rest upon, may well bear what a winged creature can. That screamer was sent to me. I wonder what has become of it. I hope it is not swept quite away."

But it would not do to sit thinking while the fire was just out, and the lamp likely to burn only an hour. She lighted the lamp with difficulty,—with a beating heart and trembling hands, lest the last available spark should go out first. But the wick caught; and the lamp was placed in the window, sending, as it seemed to Annie, a gleam through the night of her own mind, as well as through that of the stormy air. It quickened her invention and her hopes.

"There is an hour yet," thought she. "I am sure it will burn an hour; and something may be sent by that time."

She took off her cotton handkerchief, tore off the hem, and ravelled out the cotton as quickly as she could, and twisted it into a wick which she thought she could fix by a skewer across a tin cup from which Rollo drank his whisky when at home. She brought down from the chimney and looked over rapidly all the oily parts of the fish, and every fatty portion of the dried meat hung up in the smoke for winter use ; and these she made a desperate endeavour to melt in the flames of her lamp. She wrung out a few drops, —barely enough to soak her wick. This would not burn five minutes. She persevered to the last moment,—saying to herself,

"Not once for these seventeen years since I saw my husband drown, has there been a dark night between this window and the sea. Not once has my spark been put out : and I will not think it now. God can kindle fire where He pleases. I have heard tell that people in foreign countries have seen a lightning-shaft dart down into a forest, and make a tree blaze up like a torch. God has His own ways."

All the while her hands wrought so busily that she scarcely felt their aching in the cold of the night. But now her new wick was wanted, for the old was going out. It blazed up, but she saw it must soon be gone. She broke up her old stool, all shattered as it was already. Some splinters she stuck one after another into the lamp ; and then she burned the larger pieces in the hearth, saying to herself incessantly, as if for support, "God has His own ways."

But the rising and falling flame became more and more uncertain; and at last, very suddenly, it went quite out. There was not, in another minute, a spark left.

For a while there was silence in the cottage, now dark for the first time since Annie was a widow. She crept to her cold bed ; and there, under cover of the strange darkness, she shed a few tears. But soon she said to herself, "God has His own ways of kindling our spirits as well as the flame of a lamp. Perhaps by humbling me, or by changing my duty when I became too fond of it, He may warm my heart to new trust in Him. His will be done! But He will let me pray that there may be none in the harbour this night who may drown, or be buffeted in the storm because He is pleased to darken my light."

Before she had quite calmed her heart with this prayer, there was noise at a little distance, and red gleams on the fitful mist which drove past the window; and then followed a loud knocking at the door.

It was Macdonald with his people, come to see whether the lady was safe. He looked perplexed and uneasy when Annie told him that she could not think that the lady could be otherwise than safe, now she knew the places about the island so well, and was so fearless. It often happened that she was absent for a night and day; and no doubt the storm had this night detained her and her companions in some sheltered place,—some place where, she had reason to believe, they had fire and light. As for herself, when Annie saw the torch that Macdonald carried, her eyes glistened in the blaze, and she said once more in the depth of her mind,

"Surely God has His own ways."

Macdonald was very wrathful when he learned by questioning Annie how it was that her house was dark. As he hastily kindled the peats he brought in from the stack, he muttered that it seemed to have pleased God to afflict the island again with a witch, after all the pains that were taken twenty years before, as he well remembered, to clear the place of one. This woman must be a witch——

"Nay," said Annie. "I take her to be sent to us for good. Let us wait and learn."

"Good? What good?"

"It is through her, you see, that I find how kind a neighbour you are, at need," replied Annie; not adding aloud what she was thinking of,—how this night had proved that God brings help at the least likely moments.

"She is a witch," Macdonald persisted. "No power short of that could have quenched your lamp, and drawn away your only son from honouring his parent to be a slave to a stranger."

As Annie could not at the moment speak, Macdonald went on raising a flame meantime by flapping the end of his plaid.

"It is the chapel, I know. Things have never gone well for any length of time here since the chapel fell completely down, and the bleat of the kid came out from where the psalm ought to sound. We must apply ourselves to build up the chapel; and, as there is a minister coming, we may hope to be released from witches and every kind of curse."

"There will be little room for any kind of curse," thought Annie, "when the minister has taught us to 'be kindly affectioned one to another,' and not to make our little island more stormy with passions than it ever is with tempests of wind and hail."

"There, now, there is a good fire for you," said Macdonald, rising from his knees; "and I won't ask you, Annie, what was in your mind as the blaze made your eyes shine. I won't ask you, because you might tell me that I am in need of the minister, to make me merciful to a banished lady. Ah, your smile shows that that is what you were thinking of. But I can tell you this: she is a wicked woman. Her father committed murder, and she is quite able and willing to do the same thing. So I must go and find her, and take care that her foot is set in no boat but mine."

"Yours?"

"Yes. I must carry her out of the way of all boats but mine. This island was chosen for such a purpose, and now——"

"And now," said Annie, "if the lady is afflicted with such hardness of heart, is it not cruel to take her away from God's word and worship, just when there is a minister coming? Oh, Macdonald! what would you do to one who should carry away your poor sick little Malcolm to St. Kilda, just when your watching eye caught sight of an eastward sail, and you knew it was the physician coming; sent, moreover, for Malcolm's sake? What would you think then, Macdonald?"

" I should think that if Sir Alexander was in it there could be nothing done, and there ought to be nothing said. And Sir Alexander is in this, so I must go."

While Macdonald and his people were beating about among the caves, as morning drew on, Lady Carse and Rollo slipped up to the house, partly to secure a few more comforts that they had a mind for, and partly to obtain a wide view over the sea, and a certainty whether any boats were in sight.

" Have you brought up my oil can, Rollo ? " asked his mother. " If not, you must go for it, and never again touch it without my leave."

" I took it," said Lady Carse ; "and I cannot spare it."

" It cannot be spared from this room, my lady. It never left this room before but by my order, and it never must again."

" It shall never leave the place where it now is," declared Lady Carse, reddening. " I threw myself on your hospitality, and you grudge me light in the night. You, who are housed in a cottage of your own, with a fire, and everything comfortable about you—that is, every comfort that a poor woman like you knows how to value. You think yourself very religious, I am aware, and I rather believe you think yourself charitable, too ; and you grudge me your oil can, when there is no one thing on earth you can do for me but lend it."

" Your way of thinking is natural, my lady, till you

better know me and my duty. But to-day I must say that the oil can is mine, and I cannot lend it. You will please desire Rollo to bring it to me."

"I know well enough about you and your duty, as you call it. I know your particularity about a fancy of your own. I know well enough how obstinate you are about it, and how selfish, that you would sacrifice me to your whim about your duty, and your husband, and all that set of notions. And I know more. I know what it is to have a husband, and that you ought to be thankful that yours was gone before he could play the tyrant over you. You pretend to speak with authority because this cottage is yours, and your precious oil can, and your rotten old bedstead. But, besides that, I can teach you many things. You may be assured I can pay you for more oil than I shall burn to the end of my days, and for more sleeps than I hope ever to have on your old bed. You need not fear but that I shall pay for everything—pay more money than you ever saw in your life."

"Money will not do, madam. I must have my oil can. Rollo will fetch it. And you will lie down, my lady—lie down and rest on my old bed, without thinking of money, or of anything but ease to your head and your weary heart. Lie down in safety here, madam, for your head and your heart are aching sadly."

"What do you know about my head and heart aching?"

"By more signs than one. When anyone is hunted like the deer upon the hills—— "

Lady Carse groaned.

"That is only for a while, however," said Annie, tenderly. "When there is peace of mind, there is no one to hunt us— no one to hurt us. We abide here or anywhere; for the shadow of the Almighty is everywhere. No one can hunt us from it, nor hurt us within it. And I assure you, my lady, this is the place of all places for peace of mind."

"I hurt you just now, however," said the lady; "and I left you little peace of mind last night."

"If so, it must be my own fault," said Annie, cheerfully. "But never mind that. I never have any troubles now hardly; and you, madam, have so many, and such sad ones."

"That is true," said Lady Carse, as burning tears forced their way. "You never knew—you cannot conceive—such misery as mine."

Annie kissed the hand which was wet with those scalding tears, and laid her own hand on the head which was shaken on the pillow with sobs.

After a time, the lady murmured out,

"This seems very childish: but it is so long—so long since anyone—since I met with any tenderness—any affection from anyone!"

"Is that it?" said the widow, cheerfully. "Well—this is a poor place enough; and we are no companions for anybody beyond ourselves : but what you speak of is ours to give. That you may always depend on here."

"In spite of anything I may say or do? You see how hasty I am at times. Will you love me and caress me, through anything I may say or do?"

"No doubt," replied Annie, smiling. "It will be the happiest way if you constrain us to love and cherish you as your due. But if not, these are charities that God has put into every hand that is reached out to Him, that the very humblest and poorest may have the best of alms to give."

"Alms!" sighed the lady. She shook off the kind hand that was upon her aching brow, for the thought struck upon her heart that she was a destitute beggar for those smallest offices of kindness and courtesy which she had not affections or temper to reciprocate or claim.

# CHAPTER IX.

## THE COVE.

ROLLO brought word that Macdonald and his people had left the eastern caves, and were now exploring the large northern one called Asdrafil. It was time the lady was returning to her hiding place.

"O dear!" exclaimed she. "May I not rest under a roof for one night? Will Macdonald come here again so soon?"

The widow had little doubt he would. He would be popping in at all times of the day or night till he could learn where his prisoner was. She could not advise the lady to stay here, if she wished to remain on the island till the minister came.

"I must," said Lady Carse. "But I dread that cave. I hate it, with its echoes that startle one every moment, and the rough walls that look so strangely in the red light of the fire. I hate it. But," she continued impetuously, "no matter! I hate this place" (looking round with disgust). "I hate every place that I ever was in. I wish I was dead. I wish I had never been born. Now don't look at me so piteously. I won't be pitied. I can't bear to be pitied: and do you think I will let you pity me? No, indeed, I may have my own troubles. God knows I have troubles enough. But I would not change places with you—no, not

for all else that God or man could give me.   Now what are
you smiling at?   Woman, do you mean to insult my misfortunes?   I am brought low indeed, if I am to be smiled
at by a hag in a desert—I who once—O! I see; you don't
choose to yield me the small respect of listening to what I
say."

Annie was now looking round her cottage to see what she
could send down to render the lady more comfortable in
her retreat.   She tried to absorb her own attention in this
business till Lady Carse should have exhausted her anger
and become silent.   But Lady Carse once again seized the
oil can.

"Pardon me, madam," said Annie, "I cannot spare that,
as you know.   Rollo is carrying some things that I hope
may make you comfortable.   If you see anything else that
you wish for, you shall have it—anything but my lamp and
my oil."

"The oil is the only thing I want; and a small matter it
is for me, who had dozens of wax-lights burning in my
house at Edinburgh, and will have dozens more before I
die."

"Your fire must serve you, madam.   I give you what I
have to bestow.   My light is not mine to give: it belongs
to wanderers on the sea.   You cannot think, madam, of
taking what belongs, as I may say, neither to you nor me."

Lady Carse had that in her countenance at this moment
which alarmed the widow for her light; and she therefore

desired her son, with authority, to relieve the lady of the oil can, and trim the lamp ready for night.

Lady Carse, setting her teeth, and looking as malicious as an ill-bred cur, said that if the light belonged to nobody here nobody else should have the benefit of it; and attempted to empty the oil upon the hearth. This was more than Rollo was disposed to permit. He seized her arm with no gentle grasp, and saved all the oil but a few drops, which blazed amongst the peats. He moreover told the lady, with an air of superiority, that he had almost begun to think she had as much wit as the islanders; but that he now saw his mistake; and she must manage her own affairs. He should stay with his mother to-night.

It was his mother who, rebuking his incivility, desired him to attend upon the lady. It was his mother who, when Lady Carse burst away from them and said she would be followed by nobody, awoke in Rollo something of the feeling which she herself entertained.

"Carry down these things," she said. "It is too true, as she says, that every place is hateful to her; and that is the more reason why we should do what we can to make some comfort in the place she is in."

"But she says such things to you, mother! I don't want to hear any more such things."

"When people are in torment, Rollo, they do not know what they say. And she has much to torment her, poor lady! Now go; and let us try to hide her from Macdonald.

If she and the minister can have speech of each other, I trust she may become more settled in mind. You know God has made His creatures to differ one from another. There are some that sit all the more still in storms; and there are others that are sadly bewildered in tempests: but, if one ray of God's sun is sent to them, it is like a charm. They stop and watch it; and when it spreads about them, it seems to change their nature: they lie down and bask in it, and find content. It may be so with this lady if the minister gives her a glimpse of light from above."

"She shall not be carried off, if David and I can hide her," declared Rollo. "One of us must watch the Macdonalds, while the other entertains the lady."

"While she entertains you, you mean," said Annie, smiling. "She has many wonderful things to tell to such as we are."

"Not more than we have to tell her. Why, mother, she knows no more——"

"Well, well," said the mother, smiling; "you cannot do wrong in amusing her to the best of your ability, till she can see the minister, and hear better things. So go, my son."

Rollo trimmed the lanp; saw that his mother was provided with fuel and water, and departed; leaving her maternal heart cheered, so that her almost bare cottage was like a palace to her. She was singing when Macdonald put his head in, as he said, to bid her good night, but in fact to see if Lady Carse had come home.

David and Rollo acted in turn as scouts; and from their report it appeared that, though the minister's boat had not shown itself, there was a blockade of the eastern caves. The lady's retreat was certainly suspected to be somewhere in this part of the shore; for some of Macdonald's people were always in sight. Now and then, a man, or a couple of women, came prying along the rocks; and once two men took shelter in a cave which adjoined that in which the trembling lady was sitting, afraid to move, and almost to breathe, lest the echoes should betray her. The entrance to her retreat was so curiously concealed by projections of rock, that she had nothing to fear but from sound. But she could not be sure of this; and she would have extinguished her fire by heaping sand upon it, and left herself in total darkness in a labyrinth which was always sufficiently perplexing, if Rollo had not held her hand. He stepped cautiously through the sand to the nearest point to the foe, listened awhile, and then smiled and nodded to Lady Carse, and seemed wonderfully delighted. This excited her impatience so much that it seemed to her that the enemy would never decamp. She was obliged to control herself; but by the time she might speak, she was very irritable. She told Rollo not to grin and fidget in that manner, but to let her know his news.

"Great news!" Rollo declared. "The sloop which was to bring the minister and his wife was to lie-to this very night, in a deep cove close at hand; and the reason for its coming

8—2

here, instead of into the harbour, was—the best of reasons for
the lady—that Macdonald had fears that the Macleods who
manned the vessel would be friendly to his prisoner. So
the minister and his party were to be landed in the sloop's
yawl; and the sloop was to be quietly brought into the cove
after dark, that the lady, supposed to be still on the island,
might not have any opportunity of getting on board.

This did appear a most promising opportunity of deliverance. The sloop came round when expected; and, soon
after she was moored, Rollo and David went on their raft,
and spoke from it to a man who appeared to be in command, and who was, after some time, persuaded to think
that he could, for sufficient payment, go so far out of his
way as to land a lady passenger on the main—the lady being
in anxiety about her family, and able to pay handsomely for
an early opportunity of joining them. The negotiation was
rather a long one, as some of the points were difficult to
arrange; and the master of the vessel appeared somewhat
careless about the whole matter. But at last Lady Carse's
anxious ear heard the slight splash of the raft approaching
through the water; and then the tall figures of the young
men were dimly seen between her and the sky. Her tongue
was so parched that she could not speak the question which
swelled in her heart.

"Come," said Rollo, aloud. "The master will land you
on the main. You had better get on board now, before the
sea roughens. Come, they are looking out for you."

Lady Carse endeavoured to make haste; but her limbs would hardly support her. Her companions lifted her upon

ONE HELD HER STEADY WHILE THE OTHER PADDLED.

the raft, and one held her steady while the other paddled. Strong arms were ready on board the sloop to hoist her up and carry her to a heap of plaids, made into a sort of bed on deck. In another moment she sprang up, saying that she must speak to her companions one more word. A sailor who stood over her held her back; but she declared that she must thank those who had rendered her a great service. At the bidding of someone who spoke in Gaelic, the sailor withdrew his opposition, and she tottered to the side of the vessel, called to Rollo, desired him to give her love to his mother, and promised that he and David should find that she was not ungrateful.

Rollo and his comrade leaped ashore with a comfortable feeling that their business was all achieved; but yet with some little regret at losing the excitements of their late employment, and of the lady's presence and conversation. They talked her over while eating their suppers, wondered what rewards she would send, and how angry Macdonald would be; and they were about to lie down to sleep, when the night air was rent by such a scream as they had never heard. They ran out upon the rocks, and there they heard from the sloop shriek upon shriek.

"What is it?" exclaimed David. "They are murdering her!"

"No," said Rollo, after a pause. "They may be up to that, if this is a trick; but they would not do it here, nor so soon. They could do it more safely between this and St. Kilda, with a rope and heavy stone. No—they are not murdering her, whoever they may be."

"What, then? Who are they?"

"It may be a trick, and that would put the lady in a great passion; and when she is in a passion, let me tell you, not all the birds in the face of this rock can make more noise. I am not sure, but I think that is a passionate scream."

"I wish it would leave off," said David, turning away "I don't like it."

"If you don't like it," said Rollo, "I should hardly think she can. I must see about it. I think it is a trick, and that she is in a passion."

It was a trick from beginning to end. It was Macdonald's sloop; and Macdonald himself was on board, prepared to carry his prisoner to St. Kilda. The conversation overheard by Rollo in the cavern was a trick. A similar conversation had been held that day in every cave known to Macdonald along that part of the shore, in hopes of some one version being overheard by the lady's accomplices. She had fallen into the trap very easily.

"And now," said Macdonald to a clansman, "I have nearly done with the business. We have only to land her in St. Kilda; and then it will be the Macleod's affair. I shall be glad to have done with the witch. I have no wish to carry people anywhere against their wishes; and I never would, if Sir Alexander Macdonald were not in it. But I shall have done with the business presently."

# CHAPTER X.

## WHICH REFUGE?

MACDONALD'S self congratulations were premature. He
had more uneasiness to undergo about the lady than he had
suffered yet. When her screams of rage had sunk into sobs
and moans, and these again had been succeeded by silence,
he had left her undisturbed to cry herself to sleep. At daylight he had gone to take a look, but she had, as he supposed, muffled herself up in the plaids provided for her, so
as to cover her head, and thus conceal her face. But it
soon after appeared that these plaids had nothing under
them—the lady was not there.

No one had seen her move; and it must have been done
in the thickest darkness of the night. One man had heard
a splash in the water alongside. A cotton handkerchief,
which she had worn on her head, was found floating. It
was to be feared that the lady had drowned herself. After
searching about in the neighbourhood all day, Macdonald
departed in his vessel, leaving a man to watch, in case of
the body being thrown up among the rocks. He had now
no doubt of her death; and with a heavy heart he went to
confide this event—unfortunate for him, whether so or not
for anyone else—first to friends on the island, and next to
his chief. He met the minister on his landing, and took the

opportunity of whispering his news to some of those who came down to greet the pastor, to his own wife, and to Annie Fleming, desiring them not to inform the pastor, without his permission, that such a person as Lady Carse had been among them. Then he set sail for Skye, to tell Sir Alexander, with what face he might, that the poor lady would trouble them no more. It would have been a vast relief to him to have anticipated the way in which his chief would receive the news—how he would say that a great perplexity was thus solved—that no harm could ensue, as the lady was buried so long ago at Edinburgh—and that he had himself many times repented having gone into the affair, and that he never would, but for political and party reasons, and that he was heartily glad now to be quit of it, in any way—to say nothing of this being, after all, a happy event for the wretched lady herself and all belonging to her.

Meanwhile Lady Carse was not yet out of their way. She had still voice to utter political secrets, and temper all eager to punish her foes. She had slipped away in the dark, thrown herself overboard when she found Rollo below, got drenched with sea-water and bruised against the rocks, but was safe in hiding again.

Rollo's trouble was, that she laughed so heartily and so incessantly for some time, that there was danger of her merriment betraying her. He told her at last that she must try if she would leave off laughing when left to herself. If she could not, she would then, at any rate, cause no one

but herself to be taken.   He should go by a way of his own
to a point whence he could look out and see what was doing
at sea and ashore.

When he reappeared, it was with a face which would have
stopped any laughter on the side of the lady, if the laughter
had not stopped of itself long before.   She must not hope
to escape by the minister's boat.   Macdonald had so
managed his plot as to allure the lady into his boat just
when she should have been attempting to get on board the
other.   It was too late now.

The lady would not be finally convinced of this till, by
Rollo's assistance, she had reached the spot whence she
could observe the facts for herself.   The knowledge that
there was a watch set below, who would not fail to take her
alive, though his affair was to pick up her dead body, kept
her from yielding to audible grief, but never had she been
more convulsed with passion.   She pulled up the heather by
handfuls.   She dashed her head against the ground, till
Rollo restrained her.

On the dun wintry sea a vessel was sailing northwards.
It had deposited the pastor and his lady, and had actually
passed and repassed the very shore where she had been
concealed.   The long looked for vessel had come and gone.
Another was sailing eastwards in the direction she longed to
go.   This was Macdonald's ; and seeing that it was going to
Skye or the main, she now bitterly lamented having left it.
She would not believe a word about the intention to carry

her to St. Kilda. She would rather believe her own eyes, and passionately condemned herself for her haste in returning to this dreary island.

Rollo next turned her attention to the little procession which appeared upon the hills, bringing the pastor and his wife to their new abode. She looked that way; she saw the group ascending the hill—a sight so unusual in this place, that Rollo was much excited about it; but her eyes kept filling with tears, and she was so heart-sick that she could not bear any thoughts but of her own troubles. She desired Rollo to leave her. She wanted to be alone; nobody had any feeling for her; people might go and amuse themselves; all she wanted was to live and die alone.

Rollo knew that she could not do that, but he wished to go where others were going—said to himself that the lady would be the better for being left to herself for awhile, and left her accordingly. He first asked her whether he should help her down to the cave, but she made no answer, so he walked off, leaving her lying on the heather in a cold and dreary place.

She did not feel the cold, and she was too dreary within to be sensible of the desolation without. How deserted she felt as she saw Rollo walking away, quickening his pace to a run when he reached the down. It might be said that she was without a hope in heaven or on earth, but that passion always hopes for its own gratification — always expects it, in defiance of all probability, and in opposition to all reason. This is one chief mode in which the indulgence of any kind of passion is corrupting. It injures the integrity of the faculties and the truthfulness of the mind, inducing its victims to trust to chances instead of likelihood, and to dwell upon extravagances till they become incapable of seeing things as they are.

So Lady Carse now presently forgot that she was alone on a hill in a far island of the Hebrides, with no means of getting away, and no chance of letting any friend know that she was not buried long ago—and her imagination was busy in London. She fancied herself there, and, if once there, how she would accomplish her revenge. She imagined herself talking to the minister, and repeating to him the things her husband had written and said against himself and the royal family. She imagined herself introduced to the king, and telling into his anxious ear the tidings of the preparations made for driving him from the throne and restoring the exiled family. She imagined the list made out of the traitors to be punished, at the top of which she would put the names of her own foes—her husband first, and Lord Leovat next. She imagined the king's grateful command to her to accompany his messengers to Scotland, that she might guide and help them to seize the offenders. She clasped her hands behind her head in a kind of rapture when she pictured to herself the party stealing a march upon her formal husband, presenting themselves before him, and telling him what they came for

—marking, and showing him how they marked his deadly paleness, perhaps by making courteous inquiries about his health. She feasted her fancy on scenes in the presence of her old acquaintance, Duncan Forbes, when she would distress him by driving home her charges against the friends of his youth, and by appeals to his loyalty, which he could not resist. She pictured to herself the trials and the sentences — and then the executions — her slow driving through the streets in her coach in her full triumph, people pointing her out all the way as the lady who was pretended to be dead and buried, but who had come back, in favour with the king, to avenge him and herself at once on their common enemies. She wondered whether Lord Lovat's cool assurance would give way at such a moment—she almost feared not—almost shrank already from the idea of some wounding gibe—frowned and clenched her hands while fancying what it would be, and then smiled at the thought of how she would smile, and bow an eternal farewell to the dying man, reminding him of her old promise to sit at a window and see his head fall.

But the astonishment to all Edinburgh would be when she should look on triumphantly to see her husband die. He had played the widower in sight of all Edinburgh, and now it would be seen how great was the lie, and nobody could dispute that the widowhood was hers. She hoped that he would turn his prim figure and formal face her way, that she might make him, too, an easy bow, showing how she despised the hypocrite, and how completely he had failed in breaking her spirit. She hoped she should be in good looks at that time, not owning the power of her enemies by looking worn and haggard. She must consider her appearance a little more than she had done lately in view of this future time. Her being somewhat weather-browned would not matter; it would be rather an advantage, as testifying to her banishment; but she must be in comfortable plight, and for this purpose——

Here her meditations were cut short by the approach of some people. She heard a pony's feet on the rock, and caught sight of a woman's head, wrapped in a plaid, as the party mounted directed towards her. It was too late for escape—and there was no need. The woman on the pony was Annie; and nobody else was there but Rollo.

"The wonder is that you are not frozen," said Rollo, "if you have been lying here all this time. You look as red in the face, and as warm as if you had been by the fire below, in the snug sand. And that is where we must go now directly; for mother cannot stand the cold up here. She would come, as it happened she could have one of Macdonald's ponies to-day. Well, I cannot but think how you could keep yourself warm, unless you are a witch as Macdonald says you are."

"It is the mother's heart in her, Rollo, that keeps out the cold and the harm," said Annie. "It may be a wonder to you; for how should you know what it is to have had a hope of seeing one's children, to have dreamed of nothing else, waking or sleeping, and then to find it nothing but a dream. See her now, Rollo, as the cold comes over her heart. The heart can live warm on its own thoughts, when it is chilling to hear another voice speak of them."

THE WOMAN ON THE PONY WAS ANNIE.

Lady Carse was now very pale. She had once said, and then fully believed it, that she had no shame. It was long since she had felt shame. She felt it now, when it struck her that during all her long reveries about her escape and her restoration to the world, not one thought of her children had entered into the imagery of her dream. Like all people of strong passions, she had taken for granted that there was something grand and fine in the intensity of her feelings. Now, for a moment, the clear mirror of Annie's mind was held up before her own, and she saw herself as she was. For one instant she perceived that she was worthy of her husband's detestation. But she was not one to tolerate painful and humbling ideas long. She recurred to her unequalled wrongs, and was proud and comforted. She walked down to her retreat without looking behind her, leaving Rollo to tether the pony, and help his mother down as he could.

When Annie entered the cave, the drops were standing on her face, so great had been the pain to her rheumatic limbs on descending to the shore.

"But," said she, as she sank down on the sand by the smouldering fire, "I could not but come, when I heard from Rollo that you were still breathing God's air."

"Do you mean that that was good news or bad?"

"Oh, good! Surely good news. At first, for a moment after Macdonald told me you were drowned in the night, I felt thankful that your troubles were over. But I soon saw it the right way; and when Rollo whispered you were——"

"What do you mean by seeing it the right way? How do you know that your first feeling was not the right one? I am sure it was the kindest to me. You think yourself religious, and so you ought to be glad when an unhappy person is 'where the wicked cease from troubling, and the weary are at rest.'"

Annie did not reply. She was looking at the fire, and by its light it might be seen that tears were gathering in her eyes.

"Ah!" said the irritable lady, "you, and such as you, who think you abide in the Scriptures so that nothing can move you; what becomes of you when you are answered by Scripture?"

"I do not feel myself answered," Annie quietly replied.

"Oh, indeed!"

"I feel what you said out of Scripture to be quite true; and that it is a great blessing that God has set the quiet grave before our eyes for such as can find no other rest. But I would not forget that there is another and a better rest, without waiting for the grave."

"You are so narrow, Annie! You judge of everybody by yourself!"

"That is a great danger I know," Annie agreed. "And I cannot speak from my own knowledge of being troubled by the wicked. But I have read and heard much of good men who were buffeted by the wicked for the best part of their lives, and at last got over being troubled by it, and more than that."

"Ah! gloried in it, no doubt. Everyone is proud of something; and they were proud of that."

"Some such I fear there may have often been, madam;

9

but I was not thinking of those that could fall into such a snare as being proud of the ill-will of their brethren. I was thinking of some who felt the ill opinion of their brethren to be very humbling, and who humbled themselves to bear it.   Then in time they had comfort in forgiving their enemies, and at last they grew fit for a sweeter pleasure still which yet remained.   Not that, as I believe, they spoke of it, unless at moments when the joy would speak for itself; but then it has been known to burst forth from the lips of the persecuted—from some as cruelly persecuted as you, madam, that of all the thrillings that God's spirit makes in men's hearts, there is none so sweet as the first stirrings of the love of enemies."

There was no answer, and Annie went on.

"I could believe that there is no love so altogether good —at least for us here.   It is as yearning as that of a mother for her child, and as tender as that of lovers; and I should say, more holy than either, for theirs is natural to them in their mortal life, though it may be the purest part of it; the other love is an instinct belonging to the immortal life, a tongue of fire, sent down upon the head of a chosen one here and there, gifting them with the language of angels, to tell us on this side the grave what we shall find beyond. One must see that to such as these the wicked have ceased from troubling, and their weariness has long sunk into rest without help from death."

Lady Carse sighed.

"This was why I was glad, madam, to hear that death had not overtaken you yet. If you may enter into a living rest which we may see, that will, under God's blessing, be better than the blank rest of going away from your enemies, when their old wrongs may be still in your heart, making death a stinging serpent instead of a guiding dove."

Some sweet old words here occurred to Lady Carse, linked with a sweet old psalm tune—words of longing to have wings like a dove, to flee away and be at rest. She murmured these words; and they brought softening tears.

"You see, madam," said Annie, "your nest is made for you. You have been permitted to flee away from your enemies! now you are not to have wings, for the sails of the vessels are out of sight, and this makes it plain that here is to be your nest. It is but a stormy place to abide in, to be sure; but if Christ be sought, He is here to command peace, and the winds and the sea obey Him."

"I cannot stay here," sobbed Lady Carse. "I cannot give up my hopes and my efforts—the only aim of my life."

"It *is* hard," said the widow, with starting tears. "The last thing that a mother can give up,—the very last thing she can lay freely into God's hand is her yearning for her children. But you will——"

"It is not my children that I most want. You say falsely that they are the last to be given up. There is——"

"Falsely!" cried Rollo, springing to his feet. "My mother speak falsely! If you dare——"

9—2

"Gently, my boy," said Annie.    "We have not heard what the lady means."

"Be quiet, Rollo," said Lady Carse.   "Your mother speaks falsely as regards me; but I do not say that it is not after her own kind that she speaks.   If God gives me to see my children, I will thank him devoutly; but there is another thing that I want more—revenge on all my enemies, and on my husband first."

Rollo looked breathlessly at his mother.   Her face was calm; but he could see in the dim red light its expression of infinite sorrow.   She asked her son to help her to rise and go.

"I came," said she to Lady Carse, "to en'reat you to come among us, and rest in a spirit of surrender to God, on His clear showing that He chooses this to be your abiding place; and one reason for my coming was to tell you that the minister has brought his children, lest the sight of a child's face should move you too suddenly.   But I see that your thoughts are on other things; and that your spirit of surrender has yet to be prayed for.   Next Sabbath, we are to have worship once more, and ——"

"Where?"

"In the old chapel, if it can be enclosed by that time.   If not, we must wait another week: but I think it will be done. It needs but a word, madam, and the minister will ask all our prayers for one under affliction——"

"By no means.   I forbid you to speak of me, in one way

or another, to the minister or his wife. I insist on my wishes being observed in this.",

"Certainly, madam. It is not for us to interfere with your plans."

"Then go; go both of you: and do not come near me without my leave. I want to be alone—I want to be at rest; that is——"

"Ay—at rest," said Annie, half aloud. She was thinking that there would be prayers from one heart at least in the chapel for peace to a troubled spirit.

And she did not wait for the Sabbath to pray. As, assisted by her son, she painfully ascended to the heights, she saw the birds fly in and out, and hover round on the face of the precipice, as at a bidding she did not hear, she could not but silently ask that God would send His dove to harbour in the hollow of this rock with one who sorely needed a visitation of His peace.

# CHAPTER XI.

AFTER the busiest week known in the island by anybody living there, the Sabbath-day came in, calm and mild. The winters, however stormy, were never severely cold in this sea-beaten spot. It was seldom that ice was seen; and it was never more than half an inch thick. When, as on this Sunday, the wind was lulled and the sky was clear, the climate was as mild as in spring on the mainland. As soon as the aspect of the sunrise showed the experienced that the day would be fair, busy hands moved into the old roofless chapel the pulpit and benches which the pastor had brought with him—the pulpit being a mere desk of unpainted wood, and the benches of the roughest sort. For these the interior space of the old building had been cleared during the week; the floor was trodden hard and even; the walls were so far repaired as to make a complete enclosure; and some rough stones were placed as steps whereby to enter the burying-ground. Some willing hands had done more—had cleared the burying ground of stones, so that the graves, though sunk, and unmarked by any memorial but a rough and broken headstone here and there, could be distinguished by an eye interested in searching out the dead of a century ago. Another week, if sufficiently fair, was to see the walls finished and the roof on : and afterwards would be discharged the pious task of enclosing the burying-ground, and preparing room for those whom death would lay to rest in their own island. While the minister remained here, no more of the dead would be carried over the sea to some place where there was a pastor to commit them to the grave. Room was to be secured for the graves of the fifty people who were now living on the island, and for their children after them : and to all the inhabitants the island appeared a better place when this arrangement was made.

In the weak sunlight of that Sunday morning appeared gay groups of people, all excited with the great thought that they were going to the kirk. They were wonderfully well clad. How such clothes could come out of such dwellings would have been a marvel to any stranger. Festival days were so rare that a holiday dress lasted for many years. The women's cloth coats fitted at any age; and the caps with gay ribbons and bright cotton handkerchiefs did not wear out. On this remarkable day all wore their best, and a pretty sight it was to see the whole fifty people drawing towards the chapel as the pastor, his wife, and two children, issued from their lowly abode to meet the flock for the first time.

Presently the island might have appeared deserted. Far round as the eye could reach not a human being was visible outside the chapel. But something was heard which told that the place was not only inhabited, but Chris-

tianized.  The slow psalm rose into the still air.  Everyone who could speak could sing a psalm.  It was a prac-
tice lovingly kept up in every house.  Some voices were
tremulous, and a few failed; but this was from emotion.
The strongest was Annie's, for hers was the most prac-
tised.  It was her wont to sing some of the many psalms
she knew on summer days, when she sat at work on the
platform of her house, and on winter nights, when Rollo
was away.  Now that she was once more joining in social
worship, her soul was joyful, and she sang strong and
clear—perhaps the more so for the thought of the one
absent person, pining in the cavern on the shore, or
looking from afar, in desolation of heart, at the little
throng who came privileged to worship.  Perhaps Annie's
voice might unconsciously rise as if to reach the lonely
one, and invite her to come to the house of God and
seek rest.  However this might be, Annie's tones so ani-
mated some hearts and strengthened some voices as that
the psalm might be, and was, heard a long way off.  It
reached an unwilling ear, and drew forward reluctant
steps.  The links of old association, are, however, the
strongest of chains, and no charm is so magical as that
of religious emotion.  Lady Carse was drawn nearer and
nearer, in hope of hearing another psalm, till the solemn
tones of prayer reached her, and presently she was crouching
under the wall outside, weeping like a sinner who dares
not knock at the gate of heaven.

Before the service was quite finished, angry voices were heard from without, almost overpowering that of the pastor, as he gave the blessing. One of Macdonald's people, who had stepped out to collect the ponies for some of the women and children, had seen the lady, and, after one start back as from the ghost of a drowned woman, had laid hold of her gown, and said she must stay where she could be spoken with by Macdonald on his return from Skye. She struggled to escape, and did break away—not down the hill, but into the chapel.

The consternation was inexpressible. The people, supposing her drowned, took her for a ghost, though there was no ghostly calm about her; but her eyes were swollen, her hair disordered, her lips quivering with violent emotion. There was a solemnity about her, too; for extreme anguish is always solemn, in proportion as it approaches to despair. She rushed to the front of the pulpit, and held out her hands, exclaiming aloud to Mr. Ruthven that she was the most persecuted and tormented of human beings; that she appealed to him against her persecutors; and if he did not see her righted, she warned him that he would be damned deeper than hell. Mrs. Ruthven shuddered, and left her seat to place herself by her husband. And now she encountered the poor lady's gaze, and, moreover, had her own grasped as it had never been before.

"Are these children yours?" she was asked.

"Yes," faltered Mrs. Ruthven.

"Then you must help me to recover mine. Had you ever,"—and here she turned to the pastor—"had you ever an enemy?" Her voice turned hoarse as she uttered the word.

"No—yes—Oh, yes!" said he. "I have had enemies, as every man has."

"Then, as you wish them abased and tormented, you must help me to abase and torment mine—my husband, and Lord Lovat——"

"Lord Lovat!" repeated many wondering voices.

"And Sir Alexander Macdonald; and his tenant of this place; and——"

As Mr. Ruthen looked round him, perplexed and amazed, one of Macdonald's people went up to him, and whispered into his ear that this lady had come from some place above or below, for she was drowned last week. Mr. Ruthven half smiled.

"I will know," cried the lady, "what that fellow said. I will hear what my enemies tell you against me. My only hope is in you. I am stolen from Edinburgh; they pretended to bury me there——Eh? what?" she cried, as another man whispered something into the pastor's other ear. "Mad! There! I heard it. I heard him say I was mad. Did he not tell you I was mad?"

"He did; and one cannot——really I cannot——"

As he looked round again in his perplexity, the widow rose from her seat, and said,

"I know this lady; my son and I know her better than anyone else in the island does; and we should say that she is not mad."

"*Not* mad!" Mr. Ruthven said, with a mingling of surprise in his tone which did not escape the jealous ear of Lady Carse.

"Not mad, sir; but grievously oppressed. If you could quietly hear the story, sir, at a fitting time——"

"Ay, ay; that will be best," declared Mr. Ruthven.

"Let me go home with you," said Lady Carse. "I will go home with you; and——"

Mrs. Ruthven exchanged a glance with her husband, and then said, in an embarrassed way, while giving a hand to each of the two children who were clinging to her, that their house was very small, extremely small indeed, with too little room for the children, and none whatever left over.

"It is my house," exclaimed Lady Carse, impatiently. "It was built with a view to you; but it was done under my orders, and I have a claim upon it. And what ails the children?" she cried, in a tone which made the younger cry aloud. "What are they afraid of?"

"I don't know, I am sure," said their mother, helping them, however, to hide their faces in her gown. "But——"

Again Annie rose and said "There could be no difficulty about a place for the lady if she would be pleased to do as she did before—live in her cottage. The two dwellings might almost be called one, and if the lady would go home with her——"

Gratitude was showered on Annie from all the parties. As the lady moved slowly towards the widow's house, holding Annie's arm, and weeping as she went, and followed by the Ruthvens, the eyes of all the Macdonalds gazed after her, in a sort of doubt whether she were a witch, or a ghost, or really and truly a woman.

As soon as Macdonald's sloop could be discerned on its approach the next day, Mr. Ruthven went down, and paced the shore while daylight lasted, though assured that the vessel would not come up till night. As soon as a signal could be made in the morning for the yawl, he passed to the sloop, where he had a conference with Macdonald, the consequence of which was, that as soon as he was set ashore the sloop again stood out to sea.

Mrs. Ruthven and Lady Carse saw this, as they stood hand in hand at the door of the new dwelling. They kissed each other at the sight. They had already kissed each other very often, for they called themselves dear and intimate friends who had now one great common object in life —to avenge Lady Carse's wrongs.

"Well, what news?" they both cried, as Mr. Ruthven came towards them, panting from the haste with which he had ascended.

" The tenant is gone back," said he, " he has returned to Sir Alexander to contradict his last news—of your being drowned. By-the-way, I promised to contradict it, too—to the man who is watching for the body every tide."

"Oh, he must have heard the facts from some of the people at the chapel."

"If he had he would not believe them, Macdonald says, on any other authority than his. Nor will he leave his post till he finds the body, or——"

"Or sees me," cried Lady Carse, laughing. "Come, let us go and call to him, and tell him he may leave off poking among the weeds. Come; I will show you the way."

And she ran on with the spirits and pace of a girl. Mr. and Mrs. Ruthven looked at each other with smiles, and Mrs. Ruthven exclaimed, "What a charming creature this was, and how shocking it was to think of her cruel fate." Mr. Ruthven shook his head and declared that he regarded the conduct of her persecutors with grave moral disapproba- tion. Meantime Lady Carse looked back, beckoned to them with her hand, and stamped with her foot, because they were stopping to talk.

"What a simple creature she is! So childlike!" exclaimed Mrs. Ruthven.

"We must quicken our pace, my dear," replied her hus- band. "It would not be right to detain the lady when she wishes to proceed."

But now Lady Carse was beckoning to somebody else— to little Kate Ruthven, who, with her brother Adam, was peeping from the door of their new home.

"Come, Katie," said her mother, "don't you see that Lady Carse calls you? Bring Adam, and go with us."

Kate turned very red, but did not come. Lady Carse came laughing back to fetch them; but they bolted into the house, and, when still pursued, scrambled under a bed. When caught, they screamed.

"Well, to be sure," cried their mother; "what behaviour when a lady asks you to go with her! I declare I am quite ashamed."

Papa now came up, and said—

"My dears, I do not approve such behaviour as this."

Kate began to sob, and Adam followed her example.

"There, now, do not cry," said papa; "I cannot permit you to cry. You may go with Lady Carse. Lady Carse is so kind as to wish you to go with her. You will like to go with the lady. Why do you not reply, my dears. You must reply when spoken to. You will like to go with the lady—eh?"

"No," murmured Kate.

"No," whispered Adam.

"I am astonished," papa declared. "I never saw them conduct themselves in this manner before. Did you, my dear?"

"No; but it is an accident, I dare say. Something has put them out."

"I must ascertain the cause, however," papa declared. "Such an incident must not pass uncorrected. Listen to me, my dears, and answer me when I ask you a question. Look at this lady."

Kate slowly lifted her eyes, and Adam then did the same. They seemed on the verge of another scream; and this was not extraordinary; for Lady Carse was not laughing now, but very far from it. There was something in her face that made the children catch at mamma's gown.

"Listen to me, my dears," papa went on; "and reply when I ask you a question. This good lady is going to live with us——"

A deeper plunge into the folds of mamma's gown.

"And from this time forwards you must love this lady. You love this lady now, my dears, don't you?"

After as long a pause as they dared make, the children said, "No."

"Well, I never heard——!" exclaimed mamma.

"What can possess them?" inquired papa. "My dears, why do you not love the lady, eh,—Kate?"

"I don't know," said Kate.

"You don't know?—That is foolish. Adam, why do you not love this lady who is to live with us? Do not tell me that you don't know, for that is foolish. Why do you not love the lady?"

"Because I can't."

"Why, that is worse still. How perverse," he said, looking at the ladies, "how perverse is the human heart. My dear, you can, and you must do what is right. You may

love me and your mamma first, and next you must love this
lady.　Say you will try."

"I'll try," said Kate.

Adam whimpered a little longer; but then he also said,
"I'll try."

"That is right.　That is the least you can say after your
extraordinary behaviour.　Now you may go with the lady,
as she is so kind as to wish it."

Lady Carse moved off in silence; and the children,
tightly grasping each other's hands, followed as if going to a
funeral.

"Jump, my dears," said papa, when they had reached the
down.　"Jump about : you may be merry now."

Both looked as if they were immediately going to cry.

"What now, Adam ?" stooping down that the child might
speak confidentially to him, but saying to Lady Carse as he
did so, that it was necessary sometimes to condescend to the
weakness of children.　"Adam, tell me why you are not
merry, when I assure you you may."

"I can't," whispered Adam.

"You can't !　What a sudden fit of humility this boy has
got, that he can't do anything to-day.　Unless, however, it
be true, well-grounded humility, I fear——"

Mamma now tried what she could do.　She saw, by Lady
Carse's way of walking on by herself, that she was displeased;
and, under the inspiration of this grief, Mrs. Ruthven so
strove to make her children agreeable by causing them to

forget everything disagreeable, that they were soon like themselves again.    Mamma permitted them to look for hens' eggs among the whins, because they had heard that when she was a little girl she used to look for them among bushes in a field.    There was no occasion to tell them at such a critical moment for their spirits that it was mid-winter, or that whins would be found rather prickly by poultry, or that there were no hens in the island but Mrs. Macdonald's well sheltered pets.    They were told that the first egg they found was to be presented to Lady Carse ; and they themselves might divide the next.

Their mother's hope, that if they did not find hens' eggs, they might light upon something else, was not disappointed. Pephaps she took care that it should not.    Adam found a barley-cake on the sheltered side of a bush ; and it was not long before Kate found one just as good.    They were desired to do with these what they would have done with the eggs—present one to Lady Carse and divide the other.    As they were very hungry, they hastened to fulfil the condition of beginning to eat.    Again grasping one another's hands, they walked with desperate courage up to Lady Carse, and held out a cake, without yet daring, however, to look up.

"Well, what is that?" she asked sharply.

"A barley-cake."

"Who bade you bring it to me?"

"Mamma."

10

"You would not have brought it if mamma had not bid you?"

"No."

"Allow me to suggest," observed papa, "that they would not have ventured.   It would be a liberty unbecoming their years to——"

THEY TOOK TO THEIR HEELS AND SCAMPERED AWAY OVER
THE DOWNS.

"Oh, nonsense!" cried Lady Carse; "I hate these put-up manners.   No, miss—no, young master—I will not take your cake.   I take gifts only from those I love; and if you don't love me, I don't love you—and so there is a Rowland for your Oliver."

The children did not know anything about Rowlands and

Olivers; but they saw that the lady was very angry—so angry that they took to their heels, scampered away over the downs, and never stopped till they reached home, and had hidden themselves under the bed.

They were not followed. Punishment for their act of absconding was deferred till Lady Carse's errand should be finished. When once down among the rocks, Lady Carse was eager to show her dear friends all the secrets of her late hiding. As soon as Macdonald's watchman was convinced by the lady that she was not drowned, and by the minister that he might go home—as soon as he was fairly out of sight, the wonders of the caves were revealed to the pastor and his wife. The party were so interested in the anecdotes belonging to Lady Carse's season of retreat, that they did not observe, sheltered as they were in eastern caves, that a storm was coming up from the west—one of the tempests which frequently rise from that quarter in the winter season, and break over the Western Islands.

The children were aware of it before their parents. When they found they were not followed, they soon grew tired of whispering under the bed, and came cautiously forth.

It was very dark, strangely dark, till a glare of lightning came, which was worse than the darkness. But the thunder was worse : it growled fearfully, so as to make them hold their breath. The next clap made them cry. After that cry came help.

The widow heard the wail from next door, and called to

the children from her door ; and glad enough were they to take refuge with a grown-up person who smiled and spoke cheerfully, in spite of the thunder.

"Are you not afraid of the thunder?" asked Kate, nestling so close to the widow that she was advised to take care lest the sharp bone knitting needles went into her eyes. "But are not you afraid of the thunder?"

"Oh, no!"

"Why?"

"Because I am not afraid of anything."

"What, not of anything at all?"

"Not of anything at all. And there are many things much more harmful than thunder."

"What things?"

"The wind is, perhaps, the most terrible of all."

"How loud it is now!" said Adam, shivering as the rushing storm drowned his voice. When the gust had passed, the widow said,

"It was not the wind that made all that noise, it was a dash of hail. Ah! if I do fear anything, it is large hail; not because it will hurt me, but because it may break my window, and let in the wind to blow out my lamp."

"But why do not things hurt you? If the lightning was to kill you——"

"That would not hurt me," said the widow, smiling. "I do not call that being hurt, more than dying in any other way that God pleases."

"But if it did not kill you quite, but hurt you—hurt you very much indeed—burned you, or made you blind?"

"Then I should know that it was no hurt, but in some way a blessing, because the lightning comes from God. I always like to see it, because——There!" she said, as a vivid flash illumined the place. "Did you ever see anything so bright as that? How should we ever fancy the brightness of God's throne, if He did not send us a single ray, now and then, in this manner—one single ray, which is as much as we can bear? I dare say you have heard it read in church how all things are God's messengers, without any word being said about their hurting us,—'fire and hail;' here they are!"

When that gust was past, she went on,

"'Snow and vapour, stormy winds fulfilling His word.' Here we are in the midst of the fire and the hail and the stormy winds. If we looked out, perhaps we might see the 'snow and vapour.'"

The children did not seem to wish it.

"Then again," the widow went on, "we are told that 'He causeth His wind to blow, and the waters flow.' I am sure I can show you that. I am sure the sea must have risen much already, before such a wind as this. Come!" she continued, wrapping her plaid round herself and the children; "keep close to me and you will not be cold. The cold has not come yet : and if we stand under the sheltered side of the house we shall not be blown. Hark! there is the roar of the waves when the thunder stops. Now we shall see how ' He causeth His wind to blow and the waters flow."

She looked so cheerful and promised them such a sight, that they did not like to beg to stay within. Though the hail came pelting in gusts, there was no rain at present to wet them. The wind almost strangled them at the first moment; but they were under the eastern gable of the cottage in an instant, out of the force of the blast.

There they sat down, all huddled together; and there the children saw more than they had been promised.

The tempest had not yet reached Skye; and they could see, in the intervals of rolling clouds, mountain peaks glittering with snow.

"There is the snow!" said the widow. "And see the vapours!—the tumbling, rolling vapours that we call steam-clouds! Look how the lightning flash darts out of them! and how the sea seems swelling and boiling up to meet the vapours! A little way from the land, the wind catches the spray and carries it up and away. If the wind was now from the east, as it will be in spring, that spray would wash over us, and drench us to the skin in a minute."

"What, up here?"

"Oh, yes, and higher still. There! Adam felt some then."

And well he might. The sea was now wrought into such tumult that its waves rolled in upon the rocks with tremendous force, causing the caverns to resound with the thundering shock, and the very summit of the precipices to vibrate. Every projection sent up columns of spray, the sprinklings of which reached the heights, bedewing the window of the cottage, and sending in the party under the gable.

"There now," said the widow, when she had fed her fire, and sat down, "we have seen a fine sight to-day; and there will be more to-morrow."

"Shall we see it to-morrow?"

"Oh, yes; if you like to come to me to-morrow, I think I can promise to show you the shore all black with weed thrown up by the storm, and, perhaps we may get some wood. These storms often cast up wood, sometimes even thick logs. We must not touch the logs; they belong to Sir Alexander Macdonald, but we may take the smaller pieces, those of us who can get down before other people have taken them away. If the minister is not aware of this, we must tell him, and the weeds will be good to manure his kail-bed, if he can find nothing better."

"Will you go to-morrow and pick up some wood?"

"If I can get down alone; but I cannot climb up and down as I used to do. I will show you something prettier than wood or weed that I picked up, after one of these storms, when I was younger." And she took out of her chest three shells, one very large and handsome, which had been cast upon the western shore some years before. Adam thought this so beautiful that he begged to have it; but the widow could not give it away. She told him she must keep it for a particular reason; but he could see it whenever he liked to come to her for the purpose.

But Adam thought he might pick up such an one himself, if he could go to-morrow to the western shore; and his friend could not say that this was impossible. Oh! then, would she not go and show him the way? Would she not try if he and Kate helped her with all their strength? They were very strong. If she would stand up they would show her how strong they were. She stood up, and they tried to carry her. Their faces were exceedingly red, and they were very near lifting up their friend, and she was laughing and wondering whether they could carry her down the rocks in that way, when the door burst open and Lady Carse appeared.

"The children must come home," said she to Annie; "they have no business here."

"I called them in, my lady, when the thunder frightened them."

"They should not have come. They should have told you that they were under their parents' displeasure."

All now looked grave enough. The children stole away home, skilfully avoiding taking hold of the lady's offered hands. She pulled the door after her in no gentle manner. She did not much care whether the children were fond of her; but it was somehow disagreeable to her that they should be happy with her next-door neighbour.

# CHAPTER XII.

## THE STEWARD ON HIS ROUNDS.

THE return of Macdonald's boat was a great event; and especially to the inhabitants of the hill-side cottages. Macdonald was accompanied by Sir Alexander's steward, who brought some furniture and finishings for the chapel and the minister's dwelling, and, for the first time, a parcel for Lady Carse.

When the package was brought up from the shore, Lady Carse rushed in to tell Annie the news, and to bid her come and see the unpacking.

The poor lady was sure that by means of Mr. Johny, or through some other channel, tidings of her existence and banishment had reached her friends at Edinburgh, and that this parcel contained some warrant of release. With raised colour and sparkling eyes, she talked of her departure the next morning; of how it would be best to travel, when she once set foot on the main; of how soon she could reach Edinburgh, and whether it would not be better to go first to London, to lay her own case and the treason of her enemies before the Prime Minister. Mrs. Ruthven agreed to all she said. Mr. Ruthven walked to and fro before the door, stopping at every turn to offer his congratulations. Annie looked anxious and eager.

When the package was deposited before the door, and the glee of the party was at the highest, the children capered and shouted. Annie quietly checked this, and kept them by her side; whereupon Lady Carse smiled at Mrs. Ruthven, and said she pitied people who were grave when good fortune befell their friends, and who could not bear even to let children sympathize in it.

"You mistake me, madam," said Annie. "If this package was from Edinburgh, I should feel more like dancing myself than stopping the children's dancing; but I sadly fear this comes from no further off than Skye. I know the Skye packages."

"Nonsense!" cried Lady Carse. "I know nobody in Skye. I hate croakers. Some people take a pleasure in spoiling other people's pleasure."

"That is a temper that I do not approve of," observed Mr. Ruthven. "This life is to some such a vale of tears that I think it is ungrateful not to pluck the few flowers of innocent pleasure which grow by the wayside. I should think that a Christian temper would be ready to assist the enjoyment. Here, my good men——"

"What stupid fellows those men are!" cried Lady Carse. "They are actually going away without helping us to uncord the package."

She called after them; but in answer to her scolding, the men only stared; which made Lady Carse tell them they were idiots. A word or two from Annie in Gaelic brought them back directly, and obtained from them what aid was needed.

"Shall I enquire, madam," asked Annie, "anything that you may wish to know?"

"No," replied Lady Carse, sharply. "*You* speak Gaelic, I think," she said to Mr. Ruthven. "Will you learn from the men all you can about this package, and tell me every word they say?"

Mr. Ruthven bowed, cleared his throat, and began to examine the men. Lady Carse meantime said to Mrs. Ruthven, in Annie's hearing, that she must wait, and restrain her patience a little while. There was no saying what might be in the package, and they must be by themselves when they opened it.

Mrs. Ruthven said she would send the children away; and Annie offered to take them home with her.

"The children!" exclaimed Lady Carse. "Oh, bless them! what harm can they do? Let *them* stay by all means. I hope there will be nobody to spoil *their* pleasure."

Annie curtseyed, and withdrew to her own house. As she shut the door and sank into a chair, she thought how bad her rheumatic pains were. Her heart was swelling a little too; but it soon subsided as she said to herself,

"A vale of tears, indeed, is this life; or rather a waste and howling wilderness, to that poor lady with her restless mind. God knows I would not reckon hardly with her, or anyone so far from peace of mind. Nor can I wonder, when I pity her so much, that others should also, and forget other things when she is before their eyes. I did think, when I heard the minister was coming——But I had no right to expect anything beyond the blessing of the sabbath, and of burial, and the ordinances. And oh, there is the comfort of the sabbath! The Word is preached, and there is prayer and praise now on sabbath-days for a year to come; or, perhaps, as many years as I shall live. If this was a place for peace of mind before, what can trouble us now?"

The closing psalm of last sabbath had never been out of her ears and her heart since. She now began to sing it, softly at first, but louder as her soul warmed to it. She was soon stopped by a louder sound; a shrill cry from the next house, and presently Mrs. Ruthven rushed in to know what she was to do. Lady Carse was hysterical. The package had contained no news from her friends, but had brought cruel disappointment. It contained some clothing, a stone of sugar, a pound of tea, six pecks of wheat, and an anker of spirits; and there was a slip of paper to say that the same quantity of these stores would be brought yearly by the steward when he came to collect the heather rent. At this sentence of an abode of years in this place, Lady Carse had given way to despair; had vowed she would choke the steward in his sacks of feathers, that she might be tried for murder on the main; and then she had attempted to scatter the wheat, and to empty out the spirits, but that Mr. Ruthven had held her hand, and told her that the anker of spirits was, in fact, her purse—her means of purchasing from Macdonald and others her daily meat and such service as she needed. But now she was in hysterics, and they did not know what to do next. Would Mrs. Fleming come?

Annie thought the lady would rather not see her; told Mrs. Ruthven how to treat the patient, and begged that the children might be sent to her, if they were in the way.

The children were with Annie all the rest of the day; for their father and mother were exceedingly busy writing letters, to go by the steward.

In the evening the steward paid them a visit, in his round back to the boat. He was very civil, brought with him a girl, the handiest and comeliest he said, that he could engage among Macdonald's people, to wait upon Lady Carse; gave order for the immediate erection of a sort of outhouse for her stores, and desired her to say if there was anything else she was pressingly in want of. She would not say a word to him of one kind or another, but turned him over to the minister. But the minister could not carry his own points. He could not induce the steward to convey a single letter of the several written that day. The steward was sorry; had hoped it was understood that no letter was to leave the island,—no written paper of any kind,—while Lady Carse resided there. He would not take these to Sir Alexander: he would not ask him to yield this point even to the minister.

Sir Alexander's orders were positive; and it was clear that in these parts that settled the question.

While the argument was going on, Lady Carse rose from her seat, and passed behind the steward, to leave the room. She caught up the letters unperceived, and unperceived slipped them into the steward's pocket: so that while he bowed himself out, declining to touch the letters, he was actually carrying them with him.

Helsa, Lady Carse's new maid, witnessed this prank; and, not daring to laugh at the moment, made up for this by telling the story to her acquaintance, the widow, when sent for the children at night.

"That will never do," Annie declared. "Harm may come of it, but no good."

And this set her thinking.

The consequence of her meditation was that she roused the family from their beds when even Lady Carse had been an hour asleep. When Mr. Ruthven found that there was neither fire nor illness in the case, he declared to Annie his disapprobation of untimely hours; and said that if those who had a lamp to keep burning became in time forgetful of the difference between night and day, they should remember that it was not so with others; and that the afflicted especially, who had griefs and agitations during the day, should be permitted to enjoy undisturbed such rest as might be mercifully sent them.

Annie listened respectfully to all this, and acknowledged

the truth of it. It was, however, a hope that Lady Carse might possibly sleep hereafter under the same roof with her children, if this night were not lost, which made her take the liberty of rousing the minister at such an hour.

She was confident that the steward would either bring back the letters, as soon as he put his hand upon them, or destroy them; for such a thing was never heard of as an order of Sir Alexander's being disobeyed. She had thought of a way of sending a note, if the minister could write on a small piece of paper what would alarm the lady's friends. She had now and then, at long intervals, a supply from a relation from Dumfries, of a particular kind of thread which she used to knit into little socks and mittens for sale. This knitting was now too fine for her eyes; but the steward did not know this; and he would no doubt take her order, as he had done before. She believed he would come up to return the letters quite early in the morning. If she had a ball of thread ready, he would take it as a pattern; and this ball might contain a little note;—a very small one indeed, if the minister would write it.

"How would the receiver know there was a note?" asked Mr. Ruthven.

"It might be years before the ball was used up," Mrs. Ruthven observed: "or it might come back as it went."

"I thought," said Annie, "that I would give the order in this way. I would say that I want four pieces of the thread, all exactly the same length as the one that goes. The steward will set that down in his book; and he always does what we ask him very carefully. Then my relation will un-wind the ball to see what the length is, and come upon the note; and then——"

"I see. I see it all," declared Mr. Ruthven. "Do not you, my dear?"

"Oh yes; I see. It will be delightful, will it not, Lady Carse?"

"That is as it may be," said Lady Carse. "It is a plan which may work two ways."

"I do not see how it can work to any mischief," Annie quietly declared. "I will leave you to consider it. If you think well of the plan, I shall be found ready with my thread. If the steward returns, it will be very early, that he may not lose the tide."

As might be expected, Annie's offer was accepted; for even Lady Carse's prejudiced mind could point out no risk, while the success might be everything. There was some-thing that touched her feelings in the patient care with which the widow sat, in the lamplight, winding the thread over and over the small slip of paper, so as to leave no speck visible, and to make a tight and secure ball.

The slip of paper contained a request that the reader would let Mr. Hope, advocate, Edinburgh, know that Lady Carse was not dead, though pretended to be buried, but stolen away from Edinburgh, and now confined to the after-mentioned island of the Hebrides. Then followed Lady

Carse's signature and that of the minister, with the date.

"It will do! It will do!" exclaimed Mrs. Ruthven. "My dear, dear Lady Carse——"

But Lady Carse turned away, and paced the room.

"I don't wonder, I am sure," declared Mrs. Ruthven, "I don't wonder that you walk up and down. To think what may hang on this night——Now, take my arm,—let me support you."

And she put her arm around the waist of her dear friend. But Lady Carse shook her off, turned weeping to Annie, and sobbed out,

"If you save me——If this is all sincere in you, and——"

"Sincere!" exclaimed Annie, in such surprise that she almost dropped the ball.

"O yes, yes; it is all right, and you are an angel to me. I——"

"What· an amiable creature she is!" said Mrs. Ruthven to her husband, gazing on Lady. Carse. "What noble impulses she has!"

"Very fine impulses," declared the minister. "It is very affecting. I find myself much moved." And he began pacing up and down.

"Sincere!" Annie repeated to herself in the same surprise.

"Oh, dear!" observed Mrs. Ruthven, in a whisper, which, however, the widow heard: "how long it takes for some people to know some other people. There is Mrs. Fleming,

11

now, all perplexed about the dear creature. Why, she knew her; I mean, she had her with her before we ever saw her, and now we know her——Oh! how well, how thoroughly we know her—we know her to the bottom of her heart."

"A most transparent being, indeed!" declared Mr. Ruthven. "As guileless as a child."

"Call me a child; you may," sobbed Lady Carse. "None but children and such as I quarrel with their best friends. She has been to me——"

"You reproach yourself too severely, my dear lady," declared the minister. "There are seasons of inequality in us all; not that I intend to justify——"

His wife did not wait for the end, but said,

"Quarrel, my dear soul? Quarrel with your best friends! *You* do such a thing! Let us see whether you ever quarrel with us; and we *are* friends, are we not; you and we? Let us see whether you ever quarrel with us! Ah!"

Annie had finished her work; and she was gone before the long kiss of the new friends was over.

"It is only two days more to the sabbath," thought she. Then she smiled, and said, "Anyone might call me a child, counting the days as if I could not wait for my treat. But, really, I did not know what the comfort of the sabbath would be. The chapel is all weather-tight now; and thank God for sending us a minister!"

As all expected, up came the steward; very early and very angry. Nobody from the minister's house cared to

HE THREW THE LETTERS DOWN UPON THE THRESHOLD.

encounter him.    He threw the letters down upon the threshold of the door, and shouted out that his bringing them
back was more than the writer deserved.    If he had read
them, and made mischief of their contents, nobody could,
under the circumstances, have blamed him.    Here they
were, however, as a lesson to the family not to lose their
time, and waste their precious ink and paper in writing
letters that would never leave the island.

As he was turning to go away, the widow opened her
door, and asked if he would excuse her for troubling him
with one little commission which she had not thought of
the day before, and she produced the ball of thread.

Lady Carse was watching through a chink in a shutter.
She saw the steward's countenance relax, and heard his
voice soften as he spoke to the widow.    She perceived that
Annie had influence with him, if she would use it faithfully
and zealously.    Next she observed the care with which he
wrote in his note book Annie's directions about her commission, and how he deposited the precious ball in his
securest pocket.    She felt that this chance of escape, though
somewhat precarious, was the best that had yet occurred.

Before the steward was out of sight she opened the
shutter, though it creaked perilously, and kissed her hand
to the surprised Annie, who was watching her agent down
the hill.    Annie smiled, but secured caution by immediately
going in.

# CHAPTER XIII.

## TRUE SOLITUDE.

THE season advanced, bringing the due tokens of the approach of summer. The gales came from the east instead of the west, and then subsided into mild airs. The mists which had brooded over sea and land melted away, and, as the days lengthened, permitted the purple heights of the rocky St. Kilda to be seen clear and sharp, as the sun went down behind them. The weed which had blackened the shore of the island at the end of winter was now gone from the silver sands. Some of it was buried in the minister's garden as manure. The minister began to have hopes of his garden. He had done his best to keep off the salt spray by building the wall ten feet high; and it was thought that just under the wall a few cabbages might grow; and in one corner there was an experiment going forward to raise onions. Kate and Adam told the widow, from day to day, the hopes and fears of the household about this garden; and it was then that she knew that her son Rollo was now gardener, as he had been head builder of the wall.

From Rollo himself she heard less and less of his proceedings and interests. Anxious as she was, she abstained from questioning or reproving him on the few occasions when he spent an hour with her. She was aware of his high

157

opinion of himself, and of the point he made of managing his own affairs; and she knew that there were those next door who would certainly engross him if anything 'passed in his mother's house to make him reluctant to stay there. She therefore mustered all her cheerfulness when he appeared on the threshold, gave him her confidence, made him as comfortable as she could, and never asked him whence he had come, or how long he would stay. She had a strong persuasion that Rollo would discover in time who was his best friend, and was supremely anxious that when that time came there should be nothing to get over in his return to her—no remembrance of painful scenes—no sting of reproach—no shame but such as he must endure from his own heart. Strong as was her confidence in the final issue, the time did seem long to her yearning spirit, lonely as she was. Many a night she listened to the melancholy song of the throstle from the hill side, and watched the mild twilight without thinking of sleep, till was silent; and was still awake when the lark began its merry greeting to the dawn which was streaking the east. Many a day she sat in the sun watching the pathways by which she hoped her son might come to her; and then perhaps she would hear his laugh from behind the high garden wall, and discover that he had been close at hand all day without having a word to say to her. How many true and impressive things passed through her mind that she thought she would say to him! But they all remained unsaid. When the opportunity came she saw it to be her duty to serve him by waiting and loving, feeling and trusting that rebuke from God was the only shock which would effectually reach this case, and reserving herself as the consoler of the sinner when that hour should arrive.

As for the other parties, they were far too busy—far too much devoted to each other to have any time to spare for her, or any thought, except when the children were wished out of the way, or when the much more ardent desire was indulged that her house could be had for the residence of Lady Carse and her maid. In spite of all the assurances given to Lady Carse that her presence and friendship were an unmixed blessing, the fact remained that the household were sadly crowded in the new dwelling. There was talk, at times, of getting more rooms built: but then there entered in a vague hope that the widow's house might be obtained, which would be everything pleasant and convenient. At those times she was thought of, but more and more as an obstruction—almost an intruder. Now and then, when she startled them by some little act of kindness, they remarked that she was a good creature, they believed, though they considered that there was usually something dangerous about people so very reserved and unsociable.

One day this reserved and unsociable person volunteered a visit to her astonished neighbours. She walked in, in the afternoon, looking rather paler than usual, and somewhat exhausted. Mr. Ruthven was outside the door, smoking his pipe after dinner. He came in with the widow, and placed a stool for her. His wife was not in the room. Lady Carse was lying on the settle, flushed and apparently drowsy. She opened her eyes as Annie and the minister entered, and then half-closed them again, without stirring.

"Yes, I have been walking," said the widow, in answer to Mr. Ruthven's observation. "But it is not that that has tired me. I have been only as far as Macdonald's. But, sir, I must go further to-night, unless I can interest you to do what must be done without loss of time."

The minister raised his eyebrows, and looked inquiringly.

"I have learned, sir, that from this house invitations have been sent to smugglers to begin a trade with these islands, and that it is about to begin ; and that this has been done by corrupting my son. I see well enough the object of this. I see that Lady Carse hopes to escape to the main by a smuggling vessel coming to this coast. I can enter into this. I do not wonder at any effort the poor lady makes——"

"You insufferable woman !" cried Lady Carse, starting up from her half-sleep with a glowing face and a clenched hand. "Do you dare to pity me?"

"I do, madam : and I ask of you in return—I implore you to pity me. This is the bitterest day to me since that which made my boy fatherless. I have this day discovered that my fatherless boy has been corrupted by those who——"

"I do not approve of innuendo," declared Mr. Ruthven. "I recommend you to name names."

"Certainly, sir. My son has been made a smuggler by

the persuasion and management of Lady Carse; and, as I have reason to believe, sir, with your knowledge."

"Here is treachery!" cried Lady Carse. "We must make our part good. I will——I know how——"

She was hastening out, when the minister stopped her at the door. She made some resistance, and Annie heard her say something about a pistol on the top of the bed, and the wonder if her father's daughter did not know how to use it.

Even in the midst of her own grief, Annie could not but remark to herself how the lady's passions seemed to grow more violent, instead of calming down.

"You had better go, Mrs. Fleming," said Mr. Ruthven. "Make no disturbance here, but go, and I will come in and speak to you."

"How soon?" Annie anxiously enquired.

"As soon as possible—immediately. Go now, for Lady Carse is very angry."

"I will, sir. But I owe it to you to tell you that the adventure is put an end to. I have been to Macdonald's and told him, speaking as Rollo's mother, of the danger my son was in; and Macdonald will take care that no smuggling vessel reaches this coast to-night or in future."

"Go instantly!" exclaimed Mr. Ruthven, and, seeing Lady Carse's countenance, Annie was glad to hasten out of her reach.

The widow sat down on the threshold of her cottage awaiting the minister. Her heart throbbed. A blessing might be in store at the end of this weary day. Good might come out of evil. She might now have an opportunity of appealing to her minister—of opening her heart to him about the cares which she needed to share with him, and which should have been his cares as pastor. She trusted she should be enabled to speak freely and calmly.

ANNIE CLASPED HER HANDS ON HER KNEES, AND LOOKED MEEKLY
IN HIS FACE.

She prayed that she might; but her body was exhausted, so that she could not overcome to her satisfaction the agitation of her mind. It did not mend the matter that she was kept waiting very long; and when Mr. Ruthven came out at his own door, it was with some difficulty that Annie rose to make respectful way for him.

"Be seated," said Mr. Ruthven, in a tone of severity; "I have much to say to you."

Both seated themselves. Mr. Ruthven cleared his throat, and said—

"It is the most painful part of a pastor's duty to administer reproof, and more especially to members of his flock whose years should have brought them wisdom and self-control."

Annie clasped her hands on her knees, and looked meekly in his face.

"I should have hoped," Mr. Ruthven went on, "that a Christian woman of your standing, and one who is blest, as you yourself have been known to acknowledge, with a life of peace, would have had compassion on a most suffering sister, and have rather striven to alleviate her sorrows, and to soften her occasional self-reproach for what she amiably calls her infirmities of sensibility, than have wounded and upbraided her, and treacherously cut off her frail chance of release from a most unjust captivity."

"I!—I wound and upbraid Lady Carse!"

"Now, do not compel me to remind you of what you ought to know full well—the deceitfulness of the human heart. Listen to me."

Again Annie looked gently in his face.

"I left that poor lady, already overwhelmed with misfortune, prostrated anew by your attack of this afternoon. I left her dissolved in tears—shaken by agitation; and I resolved that my first act of duty should be to remonstrate privately—observe, I say privately—against the heartlessness which could pour in drops of bitterness to make the already brimming cup overflow. Now, what have you to say?"

"I should wish to know, sir, what part of my conduct it is that is wrong. If I knew this, I am sure——"

"If you knew! My good woman, this blindness and self-satisfaction appear to show that this life of peace, which you yourself acknowledge yours has been, has gone somewhat too far—has not been altogether blessed to you. If you are really so satisfied with yourself as to be unable to see any sin within you——"

"Oh, sir! Do not think me impatient if I make haste to say that I never harboured such a thought. It makes me sink with shame to think of my ever having possibly such a thought. What I asked for, sir, was to know my sin towards Lady Carse, that I might make reparation if I could, and—will it please you, sir, to tell me——"

"Tell me, rather, what sin you are conscious of; and we shall then get at the bottom of this last offence. Come, let me hear!"

Annie looked down, hesitated, blushed deeply, and said she supposed it was owing to her not being accustomed to the blessing of having a pastor that she found it so difficult to open her heart now that the blessing was given for which she had so often prayed. She would strive to overcome the difficulty. After a pause she said her chief trouble about her state of mind was that some of her trust and peace seemed to have left her.

"Ah! the moment it is put to the test!" said Mr. Ruthven.

"Just so, sir; that is what I said to myself. As long as I lived alone, out of the sound of any voice but Rollo's, I thought my peace was settled, and that I was only waiting for the better peace which is to come hereafter. Then, when Rollo was away, and my mind was searching doubtfully after him, where he might be, and whether safe or killed, I could always find rest, and say to myself that he was in God's hand, to die now or to live to close my eyes. But now, sir, there is a sadness come over me; though I am obliged to your dear children for many cheerful hours—I would not forget that. But as for my own child, when I hear his voice merry from behind your garden wall, when I have been longing for days to see his face—or when your children tell me things that he has said, just while my ear is pining for his voice, I find myself less settled in mind than I was—much less settled, sir, than I think a Christian woman ought to be."

"And this indicates more than you tell me," observed Mr. Ruthven. "What can you have done to drive your son from his home and from his mother's side? Some mistake there must be, to say the very least—some fatal mistake, I will call it, for I would not be severe—some awful mistake. Eh?"

"Perhaps so, sir." And she smothered a sigh.

The minister then gave her, at some length, his views on education, insisting much on the duty of making young people happy at home; ending with saying that no young man could, he thought, expect much comfort in the society of a mother who could be so reckless of anybody's peace as she had shewn herself that afternoon. He hoped she would take what he said in good part. It was not pleasant to him to deal rebuke · but he must not shrink from it; and he rose to go.

"Certainly, sir," said Annie, rising too, and holding by the bed to steady herself. "But, sir, if you would please to tell me particularly what you think I have done so wrong to-day——Sir, you would not have me let my son be made a smuggler?"

"You should——Nothing can be clearer than that you should——I wonder you need to be told that you should have spoken to me. Instead of which, you went quietly and told Macdonald."

"I am sure, sir, I thought you knew all about it."

"What of that? I am here at hand, to be your adviser— not to be treated with disrespect. I leave you now to think over what I have said. I trust the result will be that you will make what reparation you can to Lady Carse: though it is foolish to talk of reparation; for the mischief done is, I fear, irreparable. I leave you to think of this. Good evening!"

Annie thought of all that had passed ; and of a few other
things.   She thought that while it was clear that a pastor
might take a wrong view of the state of mind and conduct
of one of his flock, it was a privilege to know, at least, what
view he took.   He was faithful, as far as plain speaking
went : and that was much.   And then, it is so rarely that
any censure is uttered for which there is absolutely no foun-
dation, that it is usually profitable to receive it.   While feeling that "it is a small thing to be judged of man's judgment,"
it may be a great thing to know a man's unfavourable
opinion of us.   She would soon recover from this conversation ; and then, if she had obtained any wisdom from it, it
would be, after all, the marking blessing of this day.   She
was not aware of another : that Mr. Ruthven had been
somewhat touched by what she had said of Rollo—his eyes
somewhat opened.

Once more her mind rested on the idea now become so
prominent with her.   "The sabbath is coming round again,"
she thought.   "It pleases God to give us a complete blessing then.   It is His word that is spoken then—His judgment
that we are judged by.   Nothing comes between us and Him
then.   There is always the sabbath now to think of."

Tired as she was, or as she thought herself till she found
herself enjoying the repose of the moonlight shore, there
was one more walk necessary before Annie could try to sleep.

The sea was calm, and there was scarcely any wind.   If
the smuggling vessel had approached the island in any part,

it could hardly have got away again. She had not seen it from her hill-side ; but she must be satisfied that it was not on the northern shore. The western was safe enough, from its being overlooked from Macdonald's farm.

Annie had just reached the longest and widest stretch of beach when the large moon rose out of the still waters. There was not even the slightest veil of mist obscuring the horizon; and the fluctuation of the water-line was distinct upon the clear disk of the moon. The gush of quivering light which instantaneously reached from the horizon to her feet illumined Annie's heart no less than the scene around her. The ripple of the little waves which played upon the pebbles was music to her ear. In a tranquil and hopeful spirit she thought of her errand, and looked steadily over the whole expanse of the sea, where, under the broad moon-light, and a sky which had at this season no darkness in it, there was certainly no vessel in sight.

Pursuing her walk northwards, she perceived a small dark object lying on the silvery sands. When she reached it, she found it was a little cask, which the smell declared to contain rum. By the smell, and the cask being light, it was clear that some of the spirit had been spilled. Annie found a small hole, beside which lay a quill. She feared that this told too plainly of the neighbourhood of smugglers, and her heart sunk. She went on, and immediately saw another dark object lying on the beach—a person, as she thought. It was a woman, in the common country clothing, sound asleep. Annie hastened to wake her, thinking it unsafe to sleep under the moon's rays. To her extreme surprise she found it was Lady Carse.

She could imagine the lady to have come down in hope of meeting a smuggling vessel. She would not have wondered to meet her wandering among the coves; but that on such an errand, at such a time, she should be asleep, was surprising.

Annie tried gentle means to rouse her, which would enable her to slip away as the lady awoke, sparing her the pain of her presence. She rattled the pebbles with her foot, coughed, and at last sang—but all without causing the lady to stir. Then the widow was alarmed, and stooped to look closer. The sleeper breathed heavily, her head was hot, and her breath told the secret of her unseasonable drowsiness. Annie shrank back in horror. At first she concluded that much of Lady Carse's violent passion was now accounted for. But she presently considered it more probable that this was a single instance of intemperance, caused by the temptation of finding a leaking cask of spirit on the sands, just in a moment of disappointment, and perhaps of great exhaustion. This thought made Annie clear what to do.

She went back to the cask, made the hole larger with a stone, and poured out all the rum upon the sand. The cask was now so light that she could easily roll it down to the margin of the tide, where she left it, half full of sea-water. Having thus made all safe behind her, she proceeded to the

12

coves, where she found, not any signs of a vessel, but one of Macdonald's men on the watch. From him she learned that Macdonald had gone out to look for the smuggling boat; had seen it, and turned it back; and that the smuggling crew had been obliged to throw overboard some of their cargo to lighten their vessel for flight. Macdonald thought they would hardly venture hither again for some time to come. This was good news; but there was better; Rollo was not with the smugglers. He was out fowling this afternoon. Perhaps by this time he might be at home.

Annie's errand was finished; and she might now return and rest. Macdonald's man spoke of his hope of some goods being washed up by the next tide. Annie told him nothing of the cask, nor of what she had done with the rum. She commended him to his watch, and left him.

Lady Carse was still sleeping, but less heavily. She roused herself when spoken to, started up, and looked about her, somewhat bewildered

"I took the liberty, madam, of speaking to you, to waken you," said Annie; "because the moon is up, and was shining on your head, which is considered bad for the health."

"Really," said Lady Carse, "it is very odd. I don't know how I could think of falling asleep here. I suppose I was very tired."

"You look so now, madam. Better finish your sleep at home. And first, if I may advise you, you will throw some salt water on your head, and drink some fresh at the spring, when we come to it. The people here say that bathing the head takes away the danger from sleeping under the moon's rays."

Lady Carse had no objection to do this, as her head was hot; and now Annie hoped that she would escape detection by the Ruthvens, so that she alone would know the secret· Both drank at the spring, and after that it might be hoped that there would be little more smell of spirits about the one than the other.

When they passed the cask, now beginning to float in the rising tide, Lady Carse started. It was clear that she now remembered what had made her sleep. "There is a cask!" said she, in her hurry.

"Yes, a cask of sea-water," Annie quietly observed. "I emptied out the bad stuff that was in it, and——"

"You did! What right had you?"

"It was contraband," said Annie. "Macdonald saw the cargo thrown over: nobody would have claimed it, and plenty would have helped themselves to what is unfit to drink. So I poured it out upon the sand."

"Very free and easy, I must say," observed Lady Carse.

"Very," Annie agreed; "but less of a liberty than some would have taken, if I had left it to tempt them. I threw away only what is some man's unlawful property. Others would have thrown away that which belongs to God, and is very precious in His eyes—the human reason, which he has made but a little lower than the glory of the angels."

Lady Carse spoke no more—not even when they reached their own doors. Whether she was moody or conscience-stricken, Annie could not tell. All the more anxious was she to do her part; and she went in to pray that the suffering lady might be saved from this new peril—the most fearful of the snares of her most perilous life. Annie did not forget to pray that those who had driven the sufferer to such an extremity as that she could not resist even this means of forgetting her woes, might be struck with such a sense of their cruelty as to save their victim before it was too late.

# CHAPTER XIV

ONE day when Annie was trimming her lamp, she observed Helsa, Lady Carse's maid, watching the process earnestly from the door, where she was looking in. "Come in, Helsa," said the widow, in Gaelic, which was more familiar to the girl than English. "Come in, if you have nothing better to do than to see me trim my lamp."

"I am afraid about that lamp, and that is the truth," replied Helsa. "I had charge of a lamp at Macdonald's once, when my mother went to the main for a week; but then, if it went out, nobody was much the worse. If this one goes out, and anybody drowns in the harbour, and the blame is mine, what shall I do?"

"The blame yours!" said the widow, looking at her.

"Yes; when you live at Macdonald's, and I have to keep the lamp. I am not sure that I can keep awake all the night when winter comes : but they say I must."

Helsa was surprised to find that the widow knew nothing of the plan that Lady Carse now talked of more than anything else: that Annie was to go and live at Macdonald's, that Lady Carse and her maid might have the widow's house, where Helsa was to do all the work in the day, and to keep the lamp at night. The girl declared that the family never sat at meals without talking of the approaching time when they could all have more room and do whatever they pleased. Adam had cried yesterday about the widow going away; but he had been forbidden to cry about what would make Lady Carse so much happier; and when Kate had whispered to him that Lady Carse would no longer live in their house, Adam had presently dried his tears, and began to plan how he would meet the widow sometimes on the western sands, to pick up the fine shells she had told him of. Helsa went on to say that she could have cried longer than the boy, for she was afraid to think of being alone with Lady Carse at times when——"

Annie interrupted her by saying, with a smile,

"You need not have any dread of living in this house, Helsa. I have no thought of leaving it. There is some mistake."

Helsa was delighted with this assurance. But she proved her point—that the mistake was not hers—that such a plan *was* daily, almost hourly, spoken of next door as settled. She was going on to tell how her mistress frightened her by her ways : her being sleepy in the afternoons, unless she was very merry or dreadfully passionate, and so low in the mornings that she often did little but cry; but the widow checked this. While at Mrs. Ruthven's house Helsa should make no complaints to anybody else ; or, if she had serious complaints to make, it should be to Macdonald. Helsa pleaded that Macdonald would then perhaps take away the anker of spirits, as being at the bottom of the mischief; and then Lady Carse would kill her. She had once shown her a pistol; but nobody could find that pistol now. Helsa laughed, and looked as if she could have told where it was. In a moment, however, she was grave enough, hearing herself called by her mistress.

"I shall say I came to learn about the lamp," said she; "and that is true, you know."

"Why do not you speak English, both of you?" demanded Lady Carse from the door. "You both speak English. I will have no mysteries. I will know what you were saying."

Helsa faltered out that she came to see how Widow Fleming managed her lamp.

"Was it about the lamp that you were talking? I will know."

"If we had any objection, madam, to your knowing what we were saying," interposed Annie, "we are by no means bound to tell. But you are quite welcome to it. I have been assuring Helsa that there is some mistake about my leaving this house. Here have I lived, and here I hope to die."

"We must talk that matter over," declared Lady Carse. "We are so crowded next door that we can bear it no longer; and I *must* live in sight of the harbour, you know."

And she went over all the old arguments, while she sent Helsa to bring in Mr. Ruthven, that he might add his pastoral authority to her claims. After having once declared herself immovable, Annie bore all in silence; the pleas that her lamp was so seldom wanted; that it would be well tended for her, while she could sleep all night, and every night; that it had become a passion with Lady Carse to obtain this house, and that anyone was an enemy who denied her the only thing she could enjoy. These pleas Annie listened to in silence, and then to reproaches on her selfishness, her obstinacy, her malice and cruelty. When both her visitors had exhausted their arguments, she turned to Lady Carse, and intimated that now they had all spoken their minds on this subject, she wished to be alone in her own house. Then she turned to Mr. Ruthven, and told him that whatever he had to say as her pastor, she would gladly listen to.

"In some other place than this," he declared with severity. "I have tried rebuke and remonstrance here, beside your own hearth, with a perseverance which I fear has lowered the dignity of my office. I have done. I enter this house no more as your pastor."

Annie bowed her head, and remained standing till they were gone; then she sank down, melting into tears.

"This, then," and her heart swelled at the thought; "this, then, is the end of my hope—the brightest hope I ever had since my great earthly hope was extinguished! I thought I could bear anything if there was only a pastor at hand. And now——but there is my duty still; nothing can take that away. And I am forgetting that at this very moment, when I have so little else left! crying in this way when I want better eyes than mine are now for watching the sea. I have shed too many tears in my day; more than a trusting Christian woman should ; and now I must keep my eyes dry and my heart firm for my duty. And I cannot see that I have done any wrong in staying by the duty that God gave me, and the house that I must do it in. With this house and God's house——" And her thoughts recurred, as usual, to the blessing of the sabbath. She should still have a pastor in God's house, if not in her own. And thus she cheered her heart while she bathed her eyes that they might serve for her evening gaze over the sea.

She was destined, however, to be overtaken by dismay on the sabbath, and in that holy house where she had supposed her peace could never be disturbed. The pastor read and preached from the passage in the 18th chapter of Matthew, which enjoins remonstrance with sinners, first in private, then in the presence of one or two witnesses, and at last before the church. The passage was read so emphatically that Annie's heart beat thick and fast. But this did not prepare her for what followed. In his sermon the pastor explained that though the scriptural expression was, "If thy brother trespass," the exhortation was equally applicable to any Christian sister who should offend. He declared that if any

Christian sister was present who was conscious of having trespassed on the comfort and natural feelings of an afflicted and persecuted personage whom they had the honour to entertain among them, he besought the offending sister to enquire of herself whether she had not been rebuked first alone, then in the presence of a witness—alas! in vain; and whether, therefore, the time had not come for a rebuke before the Church. He would, however, name no one, but leave yet some place for repentance; and so forth.

Annie's natural dismay, terrible as it was, soon yielded before the appeal to her conscience, which the pastor supposed would appal her. She knew that she was right; and in this knowledge she raised her bowed head, and listened more calmly than many others. If there had been any doubt among the small congregation as to who was meant, Lady Carse would have dispersed it. She sat in the front row, with the minister's family. Unable to restrain her vindictive satisfaction, she started up and pointed with her finger, and nodded at Annie. The pitying calm gaze with which Annie returned the insult went to many hearts, and even to Mrs. Ruthven's so far so that she pulled the lady by the skirt, and implored her to sit down.

There are many precious things which remain always secrets to those who do not deserve to know them. For instance, tyrants know nothing of the animating and delicious reaction which they cause in the souls of their victims. The cheerfulness, sweetness and joy of their victims has ever

been, and will ever be, a perplexity to oppressors. It
was so now to Mr. Ruthven, after an act of tyranny perpe-
trated, as most acts of tyranny are, under a mistaken, an
ignorant and arrogant sense of duty. Not only did the
widow stand up with others for the closing psalm—her
voice was the firmest, sweetest, clearest in the assembly—so
sweet and clear that it came back even upon her own ear
with a sort of surprise. As for others, all were more or
less moved. But their emotion had the common effect
of making them draw back from the object of it. After
the service, nobody spoke to Annie. She heeded this
but little, absorbed as she was in thankfulness in finding
that the privileges of God's house were not disturbed—
that her relation to Him and her rights of worship were
not touched by any fallibility in His minister. As she
reached the entrance of the churchyard, Macdonald over-
took her, and made her use his arm for the descent
of the irregular steps. A few words from Helsa had put
him in possession of the case. He desired the widow not
to think for a moment of leaving her house. Everybody
wished to do what could be done to reconcile the stranger
lady to her abode in the island ; but there was a point beyond which he was sure Sir Alexander would not permit en-
croachment. His advice was to serve and please her in
small affairs, and leave it to Sir Alexander to deal with her
in such an important one as her having a house to herself.
Annie smiled, and said this was exactly her plan.

That evening was, to the inhabitants of the island, the most memorable one of the year—of the generation—of the century. This was not fully known at the time. The most memorable days often appear just like other days till they are past; and though there was some excitement and bustle this evening, no one on the island saw the full meaning of what w before his eyes.

A little before sunset, the widow plainly saw a larger vessel than often visited those seas approaching from the south-west. It was larger than Macdonald's sloop. She was straining her eyes to see whether it had two masts or three, when she heard the children's voices below. She called them up to her platform for the help of their young eyes; but when they came, they could spare little attention for the distant vessel, so full were they of the news that their mother had run down to the harbour to try to speak to some sailors who had landed from a boat which had come up the harbour while everybody was at church. It was such a pity that their father was gone, just at this time, to visit a sick person at Macdonald's farm! But their mother went directly, as fast as she could run, and Lady Carse and Helsa were to follow her as soon as Helsa had put up a bundle.

To recall Mr. Ruthven was the first thing Annie thought of. She did not venture to send the children over for him, lest their hurry and excitement, or any air of mystery, should give the alarm to Macdonald. She set out alone, doubtful as she was how and how soon she could accomplish the walk, and bitterly lamenting that her son was not within call. With her best exertions, her progress was so slow that she met the pastor a quarter of a mile from Macdonald's house.

Breathless as she was, Mr. Ruthven would have from her a full, true, and particular account of all she knew, and many declarations that she did not know as much again, before he would walk on. At last, however, he did set forth quickly on the shortest path to the harbour, while Annie turned slowly homewards over the ridge.

She was on the hill-side, not far from home, when she saw the well-known group of neighbours—the pastor's family— coming homewards, slowly and with many delays. She heard loud angry voices ; and when she approached, she saw tokens of distress in them all. Mr. Ruthven was very pale, and Helsa very red. Mrs. Ruthven was in tears, and Lady Carse's clothes and hair were dripping wet. It was clear that she had been in the water.

"Alas ! you have missed the boat !" exclaimed Annie.

Lady Carse had just lost the chance of escape, as all believed; and all were now quarrelling as to whose fault it was. Mrs. Ruthven was turning back from the shore, breathless from haste and vexation, as Lady Carse and Helsa came down. The boat, with several armed men in it, had pushed off when Mrs. Ruthven appeared. They made no reply to her signs, but lay on their oars at a little distance from the beach till Lady Carse and her maid came down. After some delay, and many signals of entreaty from the ladies, the boat again approached, and the man in command of it was told that a lady of quality, wrongfully imprisoned in this island, desired to be carried to the main, and that, once among her friends in Edinburgh, she could give rewards for her escape to any amount. There was a short consultation in the boat, a laugh, and a decisive pull to shore. A sailor jumped out and seized the lady to carry her in. Whether it was the unaccountable shout of triumph that she set up, or something else that startled the sailor, he hastily set down his burden on the rock, looked her in the face, and then spoke to his comrades in the boat. They laughed again, but beckoned him on. He placed her in the boat, but she stumbled, swayed over, caught at the side of the boat as she went over, and very nearly upset it. The men swore at her, declared her to be no lady in distress, but a tipsy gipsy, laid her down on the shore, and rowed away. Mr. Ruthven now declared that he could do nothing in such a case. Lady Carse, now sobered from everything but passion, protested that if he had had any sense or presence of mind, he might have detained the strangers till she could produce from her package proof of her rank and quality. If the wranglers could but have known who these strangers were, and whence came the distant vessel to which their boat belonged, all would have joined in thanksgiving for the lady's escape from their hands.

Annie had no more suspicion of the truth than they.

SHE SAW TOKENS OF DISTRESS IN THEM ALL.

She could only attempt to calm them, and make the best of matters by showing that possibly all might not be over yet. It was now nearly dark. If she could light two lamps for this once, it might bring back the boat. If the people on board were familiar with her light and its purpose, the singular circumstance of its being double might attract their curiosity; if strangers, they might attend to the signal from prudence.

Mr. Ruthven, being extremely cross, could see nothing but nonsense in this plan. Lady Carse, being offended with her friends, thought it the wisest and most promising scheme conceivable. Mr. Ruthven would not hear of spending a night down in the harbour, watching for a boat which would never come. To ask such a thing of him after his sabbath day's services, and all for a woman's freak, was such a thing as—as he would not describe. He could not think of doing such a thing. Lady Carse said he was no friend of hers if he did not. While Mrs. Ruthven trembled and wept, Annie said that if she could only learn where Rollo was, all would be easy. Rollo would watch in the harbour, she was sure.

Mr. Ruthven caught at this suggestion for saving his night's rest, and went off to seek Rollo; not so rapidly, however, but that he heard the remark sent after him by Lady Carse, that it was a pretty thing for a man to stand up in his pulpit, where nobody could answer him, and lecture people about Christian duty, and then to be outdone in the first trial by the first of his flock that came into comparison with him. Annie could not bear to hear this. She desired Helsa to assist Lady Carse to bed, that her clothes might be speedily dried, in readiness for any sudden chance of escape.

# CHAPTER XV.

DULL and sad was the first meal at the Ruthvens' the next morning. Lady Carse could eat nothing, having cried herself ill, and being in feverish expectation still of some news—she did not know what. Mr. Ruthven found fault with the children so indefatigably, that they gulped down their porridge and slipped out under Helsa's arm as she opened the door, and away to the next house, where the voice of scolding was never heard. The pastor next began wondering whether Rollo was still playing the watchman in the harbour—tired and hungry; and he was proceeding to wonder how a clever lad like Rollo could let himself be made such a fool of by his mother, when Helsa cut short the soliloquy by telling that Rollo was at home. He had come up just now with the steward.

"The steward," cried Lady Carse, springing to her feet. "I knew it! I see it all!" And she wrung her hands.

"What is it? my dear love, my precious friend,—what *is* the matter? Compose yourself!" said Mrs. Ruthven, soothingly.

But the lady would not hear of being soothed. It was plain now that the distant vessel, the boat, the sailors, were sent by her friends. If Mr. Ruthven had only been quick

186

enough to let them know who she was, she should by this
time have been safe.  How could they suppose that she was
Lady Carse, dressed as she was, agitated as she was !  A
word from Mr. Ruthven, the least readiness on his part,
would have saved her.  And now, here was the steward
come to baffle all.  Sir Alexander Macdonald had had eyes
for her deliverers, though her nearest friends had none.
Annie was her best friend after all.  It was Annie's ball of
thread, no doubt, that had roused her friends, and made
them send this vessel; and Annie alone had shown any
sense last night.

Mr. Ruthven did not understand or approve of very
sudden conversions; and this was really a sudden con-
version, after pointing at the widow Fleming in church
yesterday.  He ought to state too that he did not approve
of pointing at individuals in church.  He should be sorry
that his children should learn the habit; and——

"You would?" interrupted Lady Carse.  "Then take
care I do not point at her next sabbath as the only friend I
have on this island."

"My dear creature!" said Mrs. Ruthven, "pray do not
say such severe things: you will break my heart.  You do
the greatest injustice to our affection.  Only let me show
you!  If this wicked steward prevents your escape now, I
will get away somehow, and tell your story to all the world;
and they shall send another vessel for you; and I will come
with it, and take you away.  I will indeed."

13—2

"Nonsense, my dear," said Lady Carse.

"Nonsense, my dear," said the pastor.

Lady Carse laughed at this accord.  Mrs. Ruthven cried.

"If you get away," said Lady Carse, more gently, "you may be sure you will not leave me behind."

"It is all nonsense, the whole of it, about this vessel and the steward," Mr. Ruthven pronounced.  "The steward comes, as usual, for the feather-rent."

"It is not the season for the feather-rent," declared Lady Carse.

"The steward comes when it suits his convenience," decided the pastor; "the season is a matter of but secondary regard."

"You are mistaken," said the lady.  "I have lived here longer than you; and I know that he comes at the regular seasons, and at no other time."

"Oh, here are the children," observed Mrs. Ruthven, hoping to break up the party.  "My dears, don't leave the room; I want you to stay beside me.  There now, you may each carry your own porridge-bowl into the kitchen, and then you may come back for papa's and mine."

Mr. Ruthven stalked out into the garden, to find fault with his cabbages, if they were not growing dutifully.  Lady Carse stood by the window, fretted at the thick seamy glass which prevented her seeing anything clearly.  Mrs. Ruthven sat down to sew.

"Mamma," said Adam, presently, "what is a Pretender?"

"A what, my dear?—a Pretender? I really scarcely know. That is a question that you should ask your papa. A Pretender?"

"No, no, Adam. It is Adventurer. That was what the steward said. I know it, because that is the name of one of papa's books. I will show it you."

"I know that," said Adam. "But Widow Fleming called it Pretender, too."

"What's that?" cried Lady Carse, turning hastily from the window. "What are you talking about?"

The children looked at each other, as they usually did when somebody must answer the lady.

"What are you talking about?"

"The steward says the Pretender has come : and we do not know what that means."

"The Pretender come!" cried Mrs. Ruthven, letting fall her work. "What shall we do for news? Run, my dears, and ask Widow Fleming all about it. I can't leave Lady Carse, you see."

The children declared they dared not go. Widow Fleming was busy; and she had sent them away.

"Then go and tell your father. Ask him to come in."

Mr. Ruthven was shocked into his usual manners when he saw Lady Carse unable to stand or speak. His assurances that he did not believe her in any personal danger, if the report were ever so true, were thrown away. Her consternation was about a different aspect of the matter. She at once concluded that the cause of the Stuarts would be triumphant. She saw in imagination all her enemies victorious—her husband and Lord Lovat successful in all their plottings, high in power and glory; while she, who could have given timely intimation of their schemes—she who could have saved the throne and kingdom—was confined to this island like an eagle in a cage. For some time she sat paralyzed by her emotions; then she rose and went in silence to Annie's dwelling. The steward was just departing, and he seemed in the more haste for the lady's appearance; but Annie stopped him—gravely desired him to remain while she told the lady what it concerned her to know. She then said,

"I learn from the steward, madam, that it is known throughout Edinburgh that you are still in life, and that you are confined to some out-of-the-way place; though, the steward believes, the real place is not known."

"It is not known," the steward declared; "and it is anything but kind of you, in my opinion, Mrs. Fleming, to delude Lady Carse with any hope of escape. Her escape is, and will always be, impossible."

"I think it my business," said Annie, "to inform the lady of whatever I hear of her affairs. I think she ought to have the comfort of knowing that her friends are alarmed: and I am sure I have no right to conceal it from her."

The steward walked away, while the lady stood lost in reverie. One set of ideas had driven out the other. She

had forgotten all about the Jacobite news, and she stood
staring with wide open eyes, as the vision of her escape and
triumph once more intoxicated her imagination.

Annie gently drew her attention to the facts, telling her
that it was clear that the ball of thread had done its duty
well. The alarm had begun with Mr. Hope, the advocate.
He had demanded that the coffin supposed to contain the
remains of Lady Carse should be taken up and searched.
When he appeared likely to obtain his demand, Lord Carse
had avoided the scandal of the proceeding by acknowledging
that it had been a sham funeral. Annie believed that now
the lady had only to wait as patiently as she could, in the
reasonable hope that her friends would not rest until they
had rescued her.

At this moment Lady Carse's quick sense was caught by
Adam's pulling the widow's gown and asking in a whisper,
"What is a Pretender?" and by Annie's soft reply, "Hush,
my dear!"

"Hush! do you say?" exclaimed Lady Carse, with a
start. "What do you mean by saying 'hush'? Is the
Pretender come? Answer me. Has the Pretender landed
in Scotland?"

"He has not landed, madam. He is in yonder vessel.
You had a great deliverance, madam, in not being taken
away by his boat last night."

"Deliverance! There is no deliverance for me," said
the lady. "Every hope is dashed. There is no kindness

in holding out new hopes to me. My enemies will not let me stay here now my friends know where to find me. I shall be carried to St. Kilda, or some other horrible place; or, if they have not time to take care of me while they are setting up their new king, they will murder me. Oh, I shall never live to see Edinburgh again : and my husband and Lovat will be lording it there, and laughing at me and my vain struggles during all these years, while I lie helpless in my grave, or tossing like a weed in these cruel seas. If God will but grant my prayer, and let me haunt them——Stop, stop : do not go away."

"I must, madam, if you talk so."

"Stop. I want to know about this Pretender. Why did you not tell us sooner? Why not the moment you knew?"

"I considered it was the steward's business to tell what he thought proper : but I have no objection to give all the particulars. I know he whom they call Prince Charlie is in yonder vessel, which carries eighteen guns. It cannot hold many soldiers ; and Sir Alexander does not believe that he will be joined by any from his islands. He is thought to have a good many officers with him——"

"How many?"

"Some say twenty ; some say forty. It is pretty sure that Glengarry will join him——"

"Glengarry ! Then all is lost."

"Sir Alexander thinks not. He and Macleod have written

to the Lord President, that not a man from these islands will join."

"They have written to Duncan Forbes! Now, if they were wise, they would send me to him——You need not look so surprised. He is a friend of mine; and glad enough he would be at this moment to know what I could tell him of the Edinburgh Jacobites. Where is the Lord President at this time?"

"In the north, I think, preparing against the rising."

"Ay; at his own place near Inverness. If I could but get a letter to him——Perhaps he knows already that I am not dead. If I could see Sir Alexander! Oh! there are so many ways opening, if I had but the least help from any. body to use the opportunity! Sir Alexander ought to know that I am a loyal subject of King George; and that my enemies are not."

"True," said Annie. "I will endeavour to speak to the steward again before he sails, and tell him that."

"I will speak to him, myself. Ah! I see your unwilling-ness; but I have learnt—it would be strange if I had not—to trust nobody with my business. With Prince Charlie so near, there is no saying who is a Jacobite, and who is not. I will see the steward myself."

Annie knew that this would fail; and so it did. The steward's dispositions were not improved by the lady's method of pleading. He told her that Sir Alexander's loyalty to King George had nothing to do with his pledge

"DID HER FRIENDS IN EDINBURGH KNOW THAT SHE WAS ALIVE?" SHE DEMANDED.

that Lord Carse should never more be troubled by her.
He had pledged his honour that she should cause no more
disturbance, and no political difficulties would make him
forfeit his word. The steward grew dogged during the
interview.

Did her friends in Edinburgh know that she was alive?
she demanded. "Perhaps so."

Did they know where she was? "Perhaps so."

Then, should she be carried somewhere else? "Perhaps
so."

To some wretched, outlandish place, further in the ocean?
"Perhaps so."

Would they murder her rather than yield her up?
Perhaps so."

The steward's heart smote him as he said this, but he
forgave himself on the plea that the vixen brought it all
upon herself. So, when she asked the further question—

"Is there any chance for the Pretender?—any danger
that he may succeed?" the answer still was

"Perhaps so."

Mr. Ruthven, who was prowling about in search of news,
heard these last words, and they produced a great effect
upon him.

# CHAPTER XVI.

## TIMELY EVASION.

MR. RUTHVEN was walking up and down his garden that afternoon in a disturbed state of mind, when his wife came to him and asked him what he thought Lady Carse could be in want of. She was searching among his books and boxes as if she wanted something. He hastened in.

"Yes," Lady Carse replied, in answer to his question; "I want that pistol that used to be kept on the top of your bed. You need not look so frightened. I am not going to shoot you, nor anybody you ought to care for."

"I should like to understand, however," observed the pastor. "It is unusual for ladies to employ fire-arms, I believe, except in apprehension of the midnight thief: and I am not aware of any danger from burglars in these islands."

"Why no," replied the lady. "We have no great temptation to offer to burglars; and nothing to lose worth the waste of powder and bullet."

"Then, if I may ask——"

"O yes; you may ask what I want the pistol for. It strikes me that the boat from yonder vessel may possibly be sent back for me yet. They may think me a prize worth having, if the stupid people carried my story right. I would go with them—I would go joyfully—for the chance of shooting that young gentleman through the head."

"Young gentleman!" repeated Mr. Ruthven, aghast.

"Yes, the young Pretender. My father lost his life for shooting a Lord President. His daughter is the one to go beyond him, by getting rid of a Prince Charlie. It would be a tale for history, that he was disposed of among these islands by the bravery of a woman. Why, you look so aghast," she continued, turning from the husband to the wife, "that——Yes, yes. Oh, ho! I have found you out! —you are Jacobites! I see it in your faces. I see it. There now, don't deny it. Jacobites you are—and henceforth my enemies."

With stammering eagerness, both husband and wife denied the charge. The fact was, they were not Jacobites; neither had they any sustaining loyalty on the other side. They understood very little of the matter, either way; and dreaded, above everything, being pressed to take any part. They thought it very hard to have their lot cast in precisely that corner of the empire where it was first necessary to take some part before knowing what the nation, or the majority, meant to do. First, they prevented the lady's finding the pistol, as the safest proceeding on the whole; next, they wished themselves a thousand miles off, so earnestly and so often, that it occurred to them to consider whether they could not accomplish a part of this desire, and get a hundred miles away, or fifty, or twenty—somewhere, at least, out of sight of the Pretender's privateer.

In a few hours the privateer was out of sight—"Gone about north," the steward declared, "for supplies:" as nobody was willing to give them any help while under the shadow of Macdonald and Macleod.

In the evening, little Kate rushed into Annie's cottage, silently threw her arms about the widow's neck, and almost strangled her with a tight hug. Adam followed, and struggled to do the same. When he wanted to speak, he began to cry; and grievously he cried, sobbing out,

"What will you do without me? You can't see the boats at sea well now; and soon, perhaps, you will hardly be able to see them at all. And I was to have helped you: and now what will you do?"

"And papa would not let us come sooner," said the weeping Kate, "because we had to pack all our things in such a hurry. He said we need not come to you till he came to bid you good-bye. But I made haste, and then I came."

"But, my dears, when are you going? where are you going?"

"Oh, we are going directly: the steward is in such a hurry! And papa says we are not to cry; and we are not to come back any more. And we shall never get any of those beautiful shells on the long sands, that you promised me; and——"

Here Mr. Ruthven entered. He· had no time to sit

down. He told the children that they must not cry; but
that they might kiss their friend, and thank her for her kindness to them, and tell her that they should never see her
any more. There was so much difficulty with the sobbing
children on this last point, that he gave it up for want of
time, threatening to see about making them more obedient
when he was settled on the mainland. While they
clung to Annie, and hid their faces in her gown, he
explained to her that his residence in this island had
not answered to his expectation; that he did not find it
a congenial sphere; that he was a man of peace, to whom
neither domestic discord, nor the prospect of war and
difficulty without, were agreeable; and that he was, therefore,
taking advantage of the steward's vessel to remove himself
to some quiet retreat, where the pastoral authority might be
exercised without disturbance, and a man like himself might
be placed in a more congenial sphere. He was then careful
to explain that, in speaking of domestic discord, he was far
from referring to Mrs. Ruthven, who, he thought he might
say, however liable to the failings of humanity, was not
particularly open to blame on the ground of conjugal
obedience. She was, in fact, an excellent wife; and he
should be grieved to cause the most transient impression to
the contrary. It was, in truth, another person—a casual
inmate of his family—whom he had in his eye; a lady
who——

"I understand, sir.  If you will allow me to go home with you——"

"Permit me to conclude what I was saying, Mrs. Fleming.  That unhappy lady, in favour of whose temper it is impossible to say anything, has caused us equal uneasiness by another tendency of late—a tendency to indulge—— "

But Annie did not, at such a moment, stand upon ceremony.  She was by this time leading the children home, one in each hand.

"So you are really going away, and immediately?" said she to Mrs. Ruthven.

"Immediately," replied the heated, anxious Mrs. Ruthven.

"Where is Lady Carse?"

The question again brought tears into Mrs. Ruthven's swollen eyes.

"I do not know.  Mr. Ruthven wishes to be gone before she returns from her walk."

"We leave her the entire house to herself," declared the pastor, now entering.  "Will you bear our farewell message to her, and wish her joy from us of being possessor of the whole house; and of——"

"Here she comes," said Annie, quietly.  "Lady Carse," she said, "this is a remarkable day.  Here is another way opening for your deliverance—a way which appears to me so clear that you have only to be patient for a few weeks or months before your best wishes are fulfilled.  Mrs. Ruthven will now be able to do for you what she has so often longed

LEADING THE CHILDREN HOME, ONE IN EACH HAND.

to do. She is going to the main—perhaps to Edinburgh;

14

she will see Mr. Hope, and others of your friends; and tell your story. She will——"

"She will not have anything of the sort to do," interrupted Lady Carse. "I shall go and do it myself. I told her, some time since, that whenever she quitted this island I would not be left behind. I shall do my own business myself, if you please."

"That is well," interposed the pastor; "because I promised the steward, passed my solemn word to him, as a condition of my departure, that it should never become known through me or mine that Lady Carse had ever been seen by any of us. I entirely approve of Lady Carse managing her own affairs."

Annie found means to declare solemnly to Mrs. Ruthven her conviction that no such promise could be binding on her, and that it was her bounden duty to spare no effort for the poor lady's release.

She was persuaded that Mrs. Ruthven thought and felt with her; and that something effectual would at last be done.

The children now most needed her consolations.

"Do not be afraid," she said cheerfully to them. "I shall never forget you. I shall think of you every day. Whenever you see a sea-bird winging over this way, send me your love: and when I see our birds go south, I will send my love to you."

"And whenever," said Helsa, "you see a light over the

sea, you will think of Widow Fleming's lamp, won't you?"

"And whenever," said Lady Carse, with a solemnity which froze up the children's tears, and made them look in her face, "whenever, in this world or the next, you see a quiet angel keeping watch over a sinful, unhappy mortal, you may think of Widow Fleming and me. Will you?"

The awe-struck children promised, with a sincerity and warmth which touched Lady Carse with a keen sense of humiliation; not the less keen because she had brought it upon herself by a good impulse.

The pastor and his family were presently gone; and without Lady Carse. The steward guarded against that by bringing Macdonald to fasten her into her house, and guard it, till the boat should be out of reach.

Annie did not intrude upon her unhappy neighbour for the first few hours. She thought it better to wait till she was wished for.

"Our pastor gone!" thought she, as she sat alone. "No more children's voices in this dwelling! No more worship in the church on sabbaths! Thus is our Father always giving and taking away, that we may fix our expectations on Him alone. But He always leaves us enough. He leaves us our duty and our sabbaths, whether the church be open or in ruins. And He has left me also an afflicted neighbour to comfort and strengthen. Now that she thinks she

14—2

depends on me alone, I may be the better able to lead her to depend on Him."

And she was presently absorbed in meditating how best to do this most needful work.

# CHAPTER XVII.

## THE LAMP BURNS.

ANNIE had supposed that her life would be almost as quiet an one as it used to be when the minister and his family were gone. Lady Carse was her neighbour, to be sure; but every day showed more and more that even to such restless beings as Lady Carse, a time of quiet must come. Her health and strength had been wasting for some months, and now a change came over her visibly from week to week. She rarely moved many yards from the house, spending hours of fine weather in lying on the grass looking over the sea; and when confined to the house by the cold, in dozing on the settle.

This happened just when her prison was, as it were, thrown open, or, at least, much less carefully guarded than ever before. Prince Charlie's successes were so great as to engross all minds in this region, and almost throughout the whole of the kingdom. Wherever the Macdonalds and the Macleods had influence, there was activity, day and night. Every man in either clan, every youth capable of bearing arms, was raised and drilled, and held in readiness to march, as soon as arms should be provided by the government.

Annie had many anxieties about Rollo,—many feelings of longing and dread to hear where he was, and what he was

doing.   The first good news she had was that of the whole
population of Skye and the neighbouring islands, not one
man had joined the Pretender.   The news was carefully
spread, in order that it might produce its effect on any
waverers, that Sir Alexander Macdonald had written to
Lord President Forbes that not one man under him or
Macleod had joined the Pretender's army; and that he
should soon be ready to march a force of several hundred
men, if arms could be sent or provided for them against
their arrival at Inverness.   Meantime, no day passed without
the men being collected in parties, and exercised with batons,
in the absence of fire-arms.   Rollo came to the very first
drill which took place on the island; and great was his
mother's relief; and great the satisfaction with which she
made haste to equip him, according to her small means, for
a march to Inverness.

Here was an object too for Lady Carse.   She fretted
sadly, but not quite idly, about her strength failing just now
when boats came to the island so often that she might have
had many chances of escape if she could now have borne
night watching, and exposure to weather and fatigue.   She
complained and wept much; but all the time she worked as
hard as Annie to prepare Rollo for military service; for her
very best chance now appeared to be his seeing Lord
President Forbes, and telling him her story.   The widow
quite agreed in this; and it became the most earnest desire
of the whole party,—Helsa's sympathies being drawn in,—

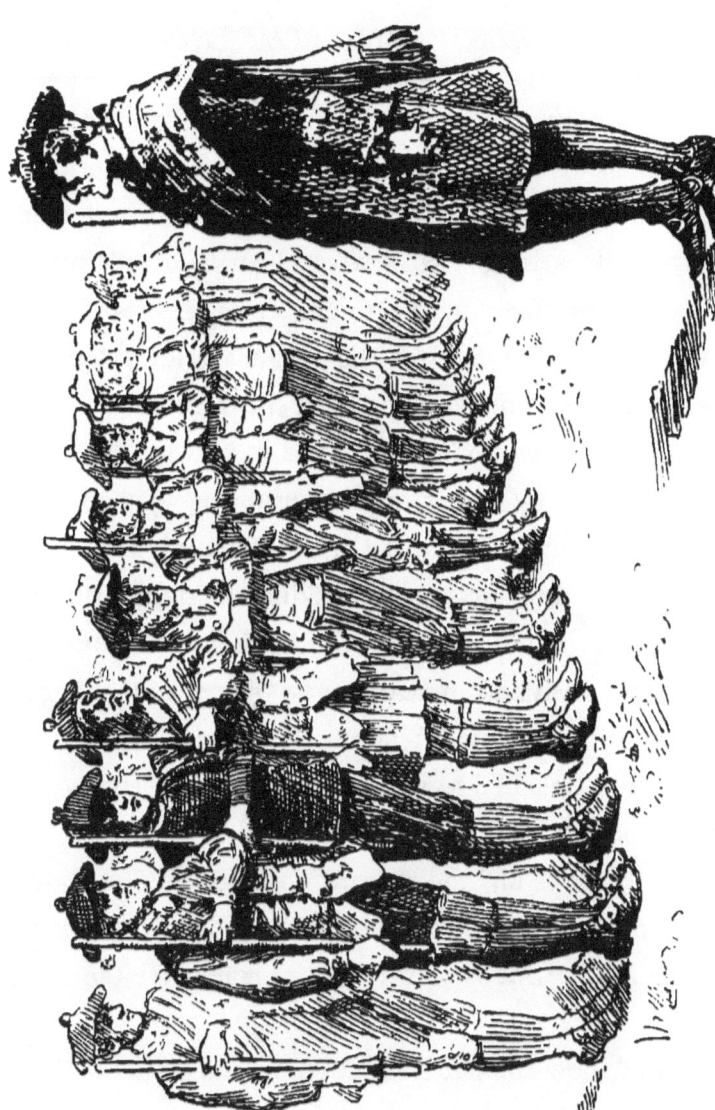

EXERCISED WITH BATONS, IN THE ABSENCE OF FIRE-ARMS.

that the summons to march might arrive. Somebody was
always looking over towards Skye; and there was so much
traffic on these seas at present, that some new excitement
was perpetually arising. Now a meal-bark arrived, telling
of the capture of others by the prince's privateer : and next
there was a seizure of fish for the king's service. Now all
eyes were engaged, for days together, in watching the man-
of-war which hovered round the coasts to prevent the rebels
being reinforced by water, and arms being landed from
foreign vessels : and then there were rumours, and sometimes visions, of suspicious boats skulking among the islands,
or a strange sail being visible on the horizon. Such excitements made the island appear a new place, and changed
entirely the life of the inhabitants. The brave enjoyed all
this : the timid sickened at it ; and Lady Carse wept over it
as coming too late for her.

"The lady looks ill," the steward observed to the Widow
Fleming, one day when, as often happened now, he came
without notice. "She is so shrunk, she is not like the same
person."

Annie told how she had lost strength and spirits of late.
She had not been down even to the harbour for two months.

"Ay, it is a change," said the steward. "I was saying to
Macdonald just now that we have been rather careless of
late, having had our heads so full of other matters. I almost
wondered that she had not slipped through our fingers in
the hurry and bustle : but I see now how that is. However,

Macdonald will keep a somewhat stricter watch; for, as I told him, it concerns Sir Alexander's honour all the more that she should not get loose, now that those who committed her to his charge are under suspicion about their politics— Ah! you see the secret is getting out now,—the reason of her punishment. She wanted to ruin them, no doubt, by telling what she knew; and they put her out of the way for safety."

"Is her husband with the Pretender then? And is Lord Lovat on that side? They are the two she is most angry with."

"Lord Carse is safe enough. He is a prudent man. He could not get into favour with the king and the minister :— they knew two much harm of him for that. So he has made himself a courtier of the Prince of Wales. He has no idea of being thrust upon the dangers of rebellion while the event is uncertain; so he attaches himself in a useless way to the reigning family. And if Prince Charlie should succeed, Lord Carse can easily show that he never favoured King George or his minister, or did them any good.—As for Lovat, he is ill and quiet at home."

"Which side is he on?"

"He complains bitterly of his son being disobedient to him, and put upon his disobedience by his Jacobite acquaintance. If the young man joins Prince Charlie, it is thought that his father will stand by King George, that the family estates may be safe whichever way the war ends.—Bless me!

what a sigh ! One would think——Come now, what's the matter ? "

" The wickedness of it ! " said Annie.

" Oh ! is that all? Lovat's wickedness is nothing new ; and what better could you expect from his son ? By the same rule, I have great expectations of your son. As you are sound, he will be sound too, and do his king and country good service. You are both on the same side, and not like the master of Lovat and his father."

" We have no estates to corrupt our minds," observed Annie. " We have only our duty to care for."

" Ay, then, you are on the same side."

" Rollo is ready to march with the men of these islands. I am on no side, sir. I do not understand the matter, and I have nothing to do with it. There is no occasion for me to take any side."

" Why yes ; as it happens, there is, Mrs. Fleming : and that is one of the things that brought me here to-day. Sir Alexander Macdonald desires that you will oblige him by not burning your lamp in the night till the troubles are over."

" I am sorry that there is anything in which I cannot oblige Sir Alexander Macdonald : but I must burn my lamp."

" But hear: you do not know his reasons. There are some suspicious vessels skulking about among these islands; and you ought to show them no favour till they show what they are "

"You do not think, sir, you cannot surely think that anybody on this island is in danger from the enemy. There is nothing to bring them here,—no arms, nor wealth of any kind;—nothing that it would be worth the trouble of coming to take."

"Oh no: you are all safe enough. No enemy would lose their time here. But that is no reason why you should give them help and comfort with your beacon-light."

"You mean, sir, that if a storm drives them hither, or they lose their way, you would have them perish. Yes; that is what you mean, and that I cannot do. I must burn my lamp."

"But my good friend, consider what you are doing. Consider the responsibility if you should succour the king's enemies!"

"I did consider it well, sir, some years ago, and made up my mind. That was when the pirates were on the coast."

"You don't mean that you would have lighted pirates to shore?"

"I could not refuse to save them from drowning: and He who set me my duty blessed the deed."

"I remember hearing something of that. But if the pirates did no mischief, your neighbours owe you nothing for that. You may thank the poverty of the island."

"Perhaps so," said Annie, smiling. "And if so, I am sure we may thank God for the poverty of the island which permits us to save men's lives, instead of letting them drown. And now you see, sir——"

"I see you are as wilful on this point as I heard you were. I would not believe it, because I always thought you a superior woman. But now—I wish I could persuade you to see your duty better, Mrs. Fleming."

"As my duty appears to me, sir, it is to save people's lives without regard to who they are, and what their business is."

"If the Pretender should come——"

"He would go as he came," said Annie, quietly. "He would get nothing here that could hurt the king, while the men of the island are gone to Inverness."

"Well, to be sure, if you would succour and comfort pirates, there is nobody whom you would not help."

"That is true, sir."

"But it is very dangerous, Mrs. Fleming. Do you know the consequences of aiding the enemy?"

"I know the consequences of there being no light above the harbour," said Annie, in a low voice.

The steward knew it was useless to say more. He thought it better to put into her hand some newspapers which contained a startling account of the progress of the rebels, embellished with many terrifying fictions of their barbarity, such as were greedily received by the alarmists of the time.

"Here," said he. "You can look these over while I go to speak to Macdonald about removing the lady to some remoter place while we have only women on the island. Pray look over these papers, and then you will see what sort of people you may chance to bring upon your neighbours, if you persist in burning your lamp. But Sir Alexander must put forth his authority—even use force, if necessary. What do you say to that?"

"Some old words," said Annie, smiling, "given to those who are brought before governors. It shall be given me in that same hour what I shall speak."

"I will look in for the papers as I return," said the steward. "You are as wilful on your own points as your neighbour. But you must give way, as you preach that she ought——"

"I do not preach that, sir, I assure you. I wish, for her own peace, that she would yield herself to God's disposal; but I would have her, in the strength of law and justice, resist the oppression of man."

The steward smiled, nodded, and left Annie to read the newspapers.

The time was short. Lady Carse was asleep; but Annie woke her, and left one paper with her while she went home to read the other. She was absorbed in the narrative of the march of the rebels southwards, and their intention of proceeding to London, eating children, as the newspaper said, after the manner of Highlanders, all the way as they went, when Lady Carse burst in, trembling from head to foot, and unable to speak. She showed to Annie a short paragraph, which told that a vessel chartered by Mr. Hope, advocate, of Edinburgh, and bound to the Western Islands, had put into the Horseshoe harbour in Lorn, to land a lady whom the captain refused to carry to her destination through a quarrel on the ground of difference of political sentiment. The lady, wife of a minister of the kirk, had sought the aid of the resident tenant to be escorted home through the disturbed districts in Argyle, while the vessel proceeded on its way—not unwatched, however, as Mr. Hope's attachment to the house of Stuart was no secret, &c., &c.

The widow was perplexed; but Lady Carse knew that Mr. Hope, her lawyer and her friend, was a Jacobite—the only fault he had, she declared. She was persuaded that the lady was Mrs. Ruthven, and that the vessel was on its way to rescue her—might arrive at any hour of the day or night.

"But," said Annie, "this lady is loyal to King George, and you reproached the Ruthvens for being on the other side."

"O! I was wrong about her, no doubt. I detest him; but she is a good creature; and I was quite wrong ever to suspect her."

"And you think your loyalty to the king would do you no harm with Mr. Hope? You think he would exert himself for you without thinking of your politics?"

"Why, don't you see what is before your eyes?" cried Lady Carse. "Is it not there, as plain as black and white can make it?"

The fact was so, though the lady's reasoning was not good. The vessel, with armed men in it, was sent by Mr. Hope to rescue Lady Carse ; and Mrs. Ruthven was to act as guide. In consequence of a quarrel between the captain and her, she was set ashore at the place where the little town of Oban has since arisen ; and the vessel sailed on out of sight. It was an illegal proceeding of Mr. Hope's, and resorted to only when his attempts to obtain a warrant from the proper authority to search for and liberate Lady Carse were frustrated by the influence of her husband and his friends.

"He will be coming! Burn the paper !" cried Lady Carse impatiently, looking from the door.

"Better not. Indeed we had better not," said Annie quietly. "They have no suspicion, or they would not have let us see the paper. They do not know that Mr. Hope is your agent ; and Mrs. Ruthven's name is not mentioned. If we do not return both the papers, there will be suspicion ; and you will be carried to St. Kilda. If we quietly return both papers, the danger may pass."

"O ! burn it, and say it was accident. How slow you are !"

"I cannot tell a lie," said Annie. "And the steward would only get another copy of the paper, and look over it carefully,—No, we have only to give him back the papers, and thank him, without agitation."

"I cannot do that," exclaimed Lady Carse. "If you will not tell a lie in such a case, I shall act one. I shall go and pretend to be asleep. I could not contain myself to speak to that man, with my deliverers almost within hearing perhaps, and that detestable St. Kilda within sight."

She commanded herself so far as to appear asleep, when the steward looked in, on his return. Annie remarked on the news of the rebels, and saw him depart evidently unaware of the weighty nature of what he carried in his pocket.

# CHAPTER XVIII.

## OPENINGS.

THE autumn of this year is even now held in memory in the island as the dearest ever known. The men were all gone to Inverness, to act under the orders of President Forbes in defending the king's cause; and the women they left behind pined for news which seldom or never came. As the days grew short and dark, there was none of the activity and mirth within doors which in northern climates usually meet the advances of winter. In the cluster of houses about Macdonald's farm, there was dulness and silence in the evenings, and anxious thoughts about fathers, husbands, and brothers, with dread of the daylight which would bring round the perpetual ineffectual watch for a boat on the waters, bearing news of the brave companies of the Macdonalds and Macleods. Sir Alexander remained in Skye, to watch against treason and danger there, while Macleod had gone with the two companies. Such a thing as murmuring against the chief was never heard of; but there were few of the women who did not silently think, now and then, that Sir Alexander might let them have a little more news—might consider their anxiety, and send a messenger when he had tidings from Inverness. This was unjust to Sir Alexander, who was no better off for news than them-

selves.   The rebels were so far successful that messengers
could not carry letters with any security by land or sea.   It
was only by folding his notes so small as to admit of their
being hidden in corners of the dress that the President could
get them conveyed to the authorities at Edinburgh ; and his
correspondence with the Government was managed by sending messengers in open boats to Berwick, whence the
garrison officer forwarded the despatches to London.   In
such a state of things, the inhabitants of remote western
islands must bear suspense as well as they could.

No one bore it so well as the Widow Fleming.   Her only
son was in one of the absent companies ; she had no other
near relation in the world ; and she had on her hands a
sinking and heart-sick neighbour, whose pains of suspense
were added to her own.   Yet Annie was the most cheerful
person now on the island.   When Helsa was fatigued and
dispirited by her attendance on Lady Carse, and was sent
home for a day's holiday, she always came back with alacrity,
saying that after all, the Macdonalds' side of the island was
the most dismal of the two.   Nobody there cared to sing,
whereas Annie would always sing when asked, and often was
heard to do so when alone.   And she had such a store of
tales about the old sea-kings, and the heroes of these islands,
and of Scotch history, that some of the younger women
came night after night to listen.   As they knitted or spun,
or let fall their work, while their eyes were fixed on Annie,
they forget the troubles of their own time, and the blasts and

rains through which they should have to find their way home.

At the end of these evenings, Lady Carse often declared herself growing better; and she then went to sleep on the imagination that she would soon be restored to Edinburgh life by Mr. Hope's means, and be happy at last. In the morning, she always declared herself sinking, and fretted over the hardship of dying just when her release was drawing near. Annie thought she was sinking, and never contradicted her when she said so; but yet she tried to bring some of the cheerfulness of the evenings into the morning. She sympathised in the pain of suspense, and of increasing weakness when life was brightening; but she steadily spoke of hope.

She was sincerely convinced that efforts which could not fail were making for Lady Carse's release, and she thought it likely that the mother and children would meet on earth, though it were only to exchange a hope that they might meet in heaven. Sincerely expecting some great and speedy change in the poor lady's fortunes, she could dwell upon the prospect from day to day with a sympathy which did not disappoint even Lady Carse. Every morning she rose with the feeling that great things might happen before night; and every night she assured her eager neighbour that no doubt somebody had been busy on her behalf during the day. Whether Lady Carse owned it to herself or not, this was certainly the least miserable winter she had passed since she had left Edinburgh.

15—2

"I am better, I am sure," she joyfully declared one night: "better in every way. How do I look? Tell me how I look."

"Sadly thin ; not so as to do justice to the good food the steward sent you," said Annie, cheerfully. "I should like to see these little hands not quite so thin."

"Ah ! that is nothing. Everybody is thin and smoke-dried at the end of a stormy winter," declared Lady Carse. "But I feel so much better ! You say it is hope ; but you see how well I bear suspense."

"I always have thought," said Annie, "that nothing is so good for us all as happiness and peace. Your happiness in hoping to see your children soon, and in obtaining justice, has done you a great deal of good ; and I trust there is much more in store yet."

"O yes; and when I get back to my friends again, I shall be happier than I was. We learn some things as we go on in life. I sometimes think that I should in some respects act differently if I had to live my life over again."

"We all feel that," said Annie.

"You know that feeling? Well, there have been some things in myself which I rather wonder at now ; some things that I would not do now. I once struck my husband."

"Once !" thought Annie in amazement.

"And I think I may have been too peremptory with the children. There was nobody then to lead me to discover such things as I do when I am with you; and I believe now that if I were at home again——I hope——I think——"

"What will you do if it pleases God to restore you to your home?"

"Why, I *have* been told that they were afraid of me at home. Heaven knows why! for I should have thought that pompous, heartless, rigid, tyrannical wretch, my husband, was the one to be afraid of; and not a warm-hearted creature like me."

"Perhaps they were afraid of him too."

"O yes, to be sure; and that is why I am here. But they need not have cared for anything I say under an impulse. They might have known that I love people when they do me justice. That, I own, I cannot dispense with. I must have justice. But if people give me my due, I am ready enough to love them."

"And how will you do differently now, if you get home?"

"I think I would be more dignified than I sometimes have been. I would rely more upon myself. I may have encouraged my enemies by letting them see how they could wound my sensitive feelings. I should not have been so ill-treated by the whole world if I had not made some mistake of that kind. I would rely more on myself, and let them see that they could not touch my peace. Would not that be right?"

"Certainly; by your having a peace which they could not touch."

There was a short pause; after which Lady Carse said, in no unamiable tone,

"I do not say these things by way of asking your advice. I know my own feelings and circumstances, and the behaviour of my family to me, better than you can do. I may be left to judge for myself; but it is natural, when a summons may come any day, to tell you what I think of the past; and of how I shall act in the time to come."

"I quite understand that," said Annie. "And I like to hear all you like to tell me without judging or advising, unless you ask me."

"Well, I fairly own to you—and you may take the confession for what it is worth—if I had to live the last twenty years over again, I should in some respects act differently, I now believe that I have said and done some things that I had better not. But I was driven to it. I have been most cruelly treated."

"You have."

"And if they had only known how to treat me! Why, you are not afraid of me, are you?"

"Not in the least."

"And you never were?"

"Never."

"Why, there now! But you are a woman of sense."

"I am not afraid of you, and never was," said Annie. looking calmly in her face; "but I can understand how some people might be."

"Not people of sense," exclaimed Lady Carse quickly.

"Perhaps not; but we do not expect all that we have dealings with to be people of sense."

"No, indeed! Nobody need ever look for sense in Lord Carse, for one. Well! I am so glad you never were afraid of me; and I am sure, moreover, that you love me: you are so kind to me!"

"I do," said Annie, smiling in reply to the wistful gaze.

Lady Carse's eyes filled with tears.

"Good night! God bless you!" said she.

"She says," thought Annie, "that I may take her confession for what it is worth. How little she knows the worth of that confession!—a confession that any acquaintance she has would blush or mock at, and that any pastor in Scotland would rebuke! but to one who knows her as I do, how precious it is! I like to be called to rejoice with the neighbours when a child is born into the world: but it is a greater thing to sit here alone and rejoice over the birth of a new soul in this poor lady. It is but a feeble thing, this new born soul—born so much too late; it is little better than blind and helpless, and with hard struggles coming on before it has strength to meet them. But still it is breathing with God's breath; and it may come freely to Christ. Christ always spoke to souls; and what were the years of man's life to Him? So I take it as an invitation in such a case as this, when He says, 'Suffer the little children to come unto

Me.' O may the way be kept clear for this infant soul to come to Him ! "

Annie had all the kindly and cheerful instincts which simple hearts have everywhere; and among them the wish to welcome the newly born with music. With the same feeling which make the people of many a heathen island and Christian country pour out their music round the dwelling which is gladdened by a new birth, Annie now sang a cheerful religious welcome to the young conscience which she trusted must henceforth live and grow for ever. Her voice was heard next door, just so as to be favourable to rest. Without knowing the occasion of the song, the lady reposed upon it; and without knowing it, Annie sang her charge to sleep, as she had often done when Rollo was an infant on her knee.

When at daylight she rose to put out her lamp, and observe the weather, she saw what made her dress quickly, instead of going to bed for her needful morning hour of sleep. A boat was making for the harbour through the difficulties of the wintry sea. It rose and was borne on the long swell so fast and so fearfully, that it appeared as if nothing could save it from dashing on the ledges of projecting rock; and then, before it reached them, it sank out of sight, to be lifted up and borne along as before. There were four rowers, a steersman, and two others, muffled in cloaks. Annie watched them till the boat disappeared in the windings of the harbour; and she was out on the hill-side, in the cold February wind, when she saw the whole party ascending from the shore, and taking the road to Macdonald's.

Here was news! There must be news. Better not tell even Helsa till she had heard the news. So the widow made what haste she could by the nearer road; but her best haste could not compare with the ordinary pace of the strangers. They had arrived long before she reached Macdonald's gate.

She walked straight in: and as she did so, one of the gentlemen who was standing before the fire glanced at another who was walking up and down.

"We need no sentinels here, my lord," said the latter in reply to the glance. "There are none but women and children on the island, and they are all loyally disposed."

"This is Sir Alexander Macdonald," said the hostess to Annie. And then she told the chief that this was the Widow Fleming, who had no doubt come to obtain tidings of her son, who had gone with the company under Macleod.

"The Lord President will give you more exact news of the company than I can," said Sir Alexander. "I only know that my people are marched to Aberdeen to protect that city from the insolence of the rebels."

The President, who was sitting by the fire, looked up kindly, and cheerfully told the widow that he had good news to give of the company from these islands. They had not been in any engagement, and were all in good health when they marched for Aberdeen, a fortnight before.

"And are they all in their duty, my lord?"

"You remind me, friend, that I ought to have put that before my account of their health and safety. They are in their duty, being proof, so far, against both threat and seduction from the rebels."

"Thus far?"

"Why, yes; I used those words because their loyalty to the king is likely to be tried to the utmost at the present time. The king's cause is in adversity, we will hope only for a short time. The rebels have won a battle at Falkirk, and dispersed the king's troops; and this gentleman, the Earl of Loudon," pointing to the one who was standing by the fire, "and I have had to run away from my house at Culloden, and throw ourselves on the hospitality of Sir Alexander Macdonald."

"And what will become of your house, my lord?"

"I have thrown my house and fortune into the cause, as you have thrown something much more important—your son. If you can wait God's disposal cheerfully, much more should I. I cannot bestow a thought on my house."

"Except," said Sir Alexander, "that you have nothing else to think about here; and nothing to do but to think, for this day, at least. We must remain here. So safe as it is, in comparison with any part of Skye, or even Barra, I should recommend your staying here till we have some assurance of safety elsewhere."

" I will venture to offer something for the Lord President to think of and to do," said the widow, coming forward with an earnestness which fixed everybody's attention at once, and made Sir Alexander stop in his walk. He was about to command silence on Annie's part, but a glance at her face showed him that this would be useless.

" Let me first be sure that I am right," said Annie. " Is the Lord President whom I speak to named Duncan Forbes? And is he a friend of Lord Carse?"

" I am Duncan Forbes, and Lord Carse is an acquaintance of mine."

" Has he ever told you that his unhappy wife is not dead, as he pretended, but living in miserable banishment on this island?"

" On this island! Nonsense!" cried Sir Alexander.

When assured by the hostess and Annie that it was so, he swore at his steward, his tenant, and himself. On first hearing of the alarm being taken by the lady's friends at Edinburgh, he had ordered her removal to St. Kilda, and had supposed it effected long ago. The troubles of the time, which left no boat or men disposable, had caused the delay; and now, between his rage at any command of his having been disregarded, and his sense of his absurdity in bringing a friend of his prisoner to her very door, he was perfectly exasperated. He muttered curses as he strode up and down.

Meantime the Lord President was quietly preparing himself for a walk. Everybody but Annie entreated him to stay till he had breakfasted, and warmed himself, Lord Loudon adding that the lady would not fly away in the course of the next hour if she had been detained so many years. It did not escape the President's observant eye that these words struck Sir Alexander, and that he made a movement towards the door. There being a boat and rowers at hand, she might be found to have flown within the hour, if he stayed to breakfast.

He approached Sir Alexander, and laid his hand on his arm, saying—

" My good friend, I advise you to yield up this affair into my hands as the first law officer of Scotland. All chance of concealment of this lady's case has been over for some time. Measures have been taken for some months to compel you to resign the charge which you surely cannot wish to retain—— "

Sir Alexander broke in with curses on himself for having ever been persuaded into involving himself in such a business.

" By the desire, I presume, of Lord Carse, Lord Lovat, Mr. Forster, and others, not now particularly distinguished for their loyalty."

" That is the cursed part of it," muttered Sir Alexander.

"It was to further their Jacobite plots that they put this vixen out of the way, because she had some secrets in her power, and they laid it all on her temper, which, they told me, caused my lord to go in fear of his reputation and his life."

"There was truth in that, to my knowledge," observed the President; "and there were considerations connected with the daughters—natural considerations, though leading to unnatural cruelty."

"Politics were at the bottom, for all that," said the chief, "And now, as she has been my prisoner for so long, I suppose they will throw the whole responsibility upon me. The rebel leaders hate me for my loyalty as they hate the devil. They hate me——"

"As they hate Lord Loudon and myself," interposed the President, "which they do, I take it, much more bitterly than they ever did the devil. But, Sir Alexander, let me point out to you that your course in regard to this lady is now clear. If the rebellion succeeds, let the leaders find that you have taken out of their hands this weapon, which they might otherwise use for your destruction. Let them find you acting with me in restoring the lady to her rights. If, as I anticipate, the rebellion is yet to fail, this is still your only safe course. It will afford you the best chance of impunity—which impunity, however, it is not for me to promise—for the illegality and the guilt of your past conduct to the victim. There is something in our friend's countenance here," he continued, turning to the widow with a smile, "which I should like to understand. I fear I have not her good opinion, as I could wish."

Annie told exactly what she was thinking : that all this reasoning was wrong, because wasteful of the right. Surely it was the shortest and clearest thing to say that, late as it was, it was better for Sir Alexander to begin doing right than persist in the wrong.

"I quite agree with you," said the President, "and if people generally were like you, we should be saved most of the argumentation of our law courts—if, indeed, we should need the courts at all, or, perhaps, even any human law. Come, Sir Alexander, let me beg your company to call on Lady Carse. One needs the countenance of the chief, who is always and everywhere welcome in his own territory, to excuse so early a visit."

Sir Alexander positively declined going. He was, in truth, afraid of the lady's tongue in the presence of a legal functionary, before whom he could neither order nor threaten violence.

It was a great relief to Annie that he did not go. . She needed the opportunity of the walk to prepare the President to meet his old acquaintance, and to speak wisely to her.

Even the President, with his habitual self-possession, could not conceal his embarrassment at the change in Lady Carse. The light from the window shone upon her face ; yet he glanced at the widow, as in doubt whether this could be the right person, before he made his complaints. In the midst of her agitation at the meeting, Lady Carse said to herself that the good man was losing his memory; and, indeed, it was time; for he must be above sixty. She wondered whether it was a sign that her husband might be losing his faculties too : but she feared Duncan Forbes was a good deal the older of the two.

It would have astonished those who did not know Duncan Forbes to see him now. He was a fugitive from the rebels, who might at the moment be burning his house, and impoverishing his tenants; he had been wandering in the mountains for many days, and had spent the last night upon the sea; his clothes were weather-stained, his periwig damp, and his buckles rusted; he was at the moment weary and aching with cold and hunger; he was in the presence of a lady whom he had for years supposed dead and buried; and he was under the shock of seeing a face once full of health and animation now not only wasted, but alive with misery in every fibre : yet he sat on a bench in this island dwelling —in his eyes a hovel—with his gold-headed cane between his knees, talking with all the courtesy, calmness, and measured cheerfulness, which Edinburgh knew so well. Nothing could be better for Lady Carse than his manner. It actually took away the sense of wonder at their meeting; and meeting thus. While he had stood at the threshold, and she heard whom she was to see, her brain had reeled, and her countenance had become such as it might well dismay him to see; but such was the influence of his composure, and of the associations which his presence revived, that she soon appeared in Annie's eyes a totally altered person. As the two sat at breakfast, Annie saw before her the gentleman and lady complete, in spite of every disguise of dress and circumstance.

At the close of the meal, Annie slipped away to her own house: but it was not long before she was sent for, at the desire, not of Lady Carse, but of the President. He wished her to hear what he had to relate. He told of Mr. Hope's exertions in Edinburgh, and of his having at length ventured upon an illegal proceeding for which only the disturbance of the times could be pleaded in excuse. He had sent out a vessel, containing a few armed men, and Mrs. Ruthven, who had undertaken to act as guide to Lady Carse's residence. It was understood that the captain had set Mrs. Ruthven ashore in Lorn, through some disagreement between them; and that the vessel had proceeded as far as Barra, when the captain was so certainly informed that the lady had been removed to the mainland that he turned back; pleading, further, that there was such evident want of sense in Mrs. Ruthven, and such contradictory testimony between her and her husband, that he doubted whether any portion of their story was true. It was next believed that a commission of enquiry would be soon sent to this and other islands: but this could not take place until the public tranquility should be in some degree restored.

"Before that, I shall be dead," sighed Lady Carse, impatiently.

"There is no need now to wait for the commission," said the President. "Where I am, all violations of the law must cease. Your captivity is now at an end, except in so far as you are subject to ill health, or, like myself, to winter weather and most wintry fortunes."

THE TWO SAT AT BREAKFAST.

"The day is come, then," said Annie, through shining tears. "You are now delivered out of the hand of man, and have to wait only God's pleasure."

"What matters it," murmured Lady Carse, "how you call my misfortunes? Here I sit, a shivering exile——"

16

"So far like myself," observed the President, moving nearer the scanty fire.

"You have not been heart-sick for years under insufferable wrongs," declared Lady Carse. "And you have not the grave open at your feet while everything you care for is beckoning to you to come away. You——"

"Pardon me, my old friend," said he, mildly. "That is exactly my case. I am old : the grave is open at my feet; and beyond it stands she who, though early lost, has been the constant passion of my life. Perhaps my heart may have pined under the privation of her society as sensibly as yours under afflictions more strange in the eyes of the world. But it is not wise—it does not give strength, but impair it— thus to·compare human afflictions. I should prefer cheerfully encouraging each other to wait for release; I see little prospect of any release this day for us exiles ; so let me see what my memory is worth in my old age—let me see what I can recall of our Janet. You know I always consider Janet my own by favouritism ; and she called me grandfather the last time we met, as she used to do before she was able to spell so long a word."

He told so much of Janet, that Lady Carse changed her opinion about his loss of memory. Again Annie stole home : and there did the President seek her, after a long conversation with her neighbour.

"I wish to know," said he, "whether the great change that I observe in this lady is recent."

"She is greatly changed within a few months," replied the widow: "and I think she has sunk within a few days. I see, sir, that you look for her release soon."

"If the change has been rapid of late," he replied, "it is my opinion that she is dying."

"Is there anything that you would wish done?" asked Annie.

"What can we do? I perceive that she is in possession of what is perhaps the only aid her case admits of—a friend who can at once soothe her earthly life, and feed her heavenly one."

Annie bowed her head, and then said—

"You would not have me conceal her state from herself, I think, sir."

"I would not. I believe she is aware that I think her very ill—decisively ill.

"I hope she is. I have seen in her of late that which makes me desire for her the happy knowledge that she is going home to a place where she may find more peace than near her enemies in a city of the earth." Fancying that the President shook his head, Annie went on—

"I would not be presumptuous, sir, for another any more than for myself: but when a better life is permitted to begin, ever so feebly, here, surely God sends death, not to put it out, but to remove it to a safer place."

The President smiled kindly, and walked away.

# CHAPTER XIX.

SIR ALEXANDER and his guests remained on the island
only a few days; but during that time the President gave
Lady Carse many hours of his society. Full as his mind
was of public and private affairs—charged as he was with
the defence of Scotland against the treason of the Pretender
and his followers—grieved as he was by the heart-sorrows
which attend civil war—and now a fugitive, destitute of
means, and in peril of his life—he still had cheerfulness
and patience to minister to Lady Carse. From his
deliberate and courteous entrance, his air of leisure, his
quiet humour in conversation, and his clear remembrance of
small incidents relating to the lady's family and acquaintance, anyone would have supposed that he had not a care
in the world. For the hour, Lady Carse almost felt as if
she had none. She declared herself getting quite well; and
she did strive, by a self-command and prudence such as
astonished even Annie, to gain such ground as should
enable her to leave the island when the President did—that
is, as she and others supposed, when the spring should
favour the sending an English army to contest the empire
once more with the still successful Pretender.

But, in four days, there was a sudden break up. A

236

faithful boatman of Sir Alexander's came over from Skye to give warning of danger. There were no three men in Scotland so hated by the rebels as the three gentlemen now on the island; and no expense or pains were to be spared in capturing them. They must not remain, from any mere hope of secrecy, in a place which contained only women and children. They must go where they could not only hide, but be guarded by fighting men. It was decided to be off that very moment. The President desired one half-hour, that he might see Lady Carse, and assure her of his care and protection, and of relief, as soon as he could command the means. He entered as deliberately as usual, and merely looked at his watch and said that he had ten minutes, and no more.

"You must not go," said she. "We cannot spare you. Oh, you need not fear any danger! We have admirable hiding-places in our rock, where, to my knowledge, you can have good fires, and a soft bed of warm sand. You are better here. You must not go."

Of course the President said he must, and civilly stopped the remonstrance. Then she declared, with a forced quietness,

"If you will go, I must go with you. Do not say a word against it. I have your promise, and I will hold you to it. Oh, yes, I am fit to go—fitter than to stay. If I stay, I shall die this night. If I go, I shall live to keep a certain promise of mine—to go and see my Lord Lovat's head fall.

I will not detain you; we have five minutes of your ten yet.
I will be across the threshold before your ten minutes are
up.  Helsa!  Helsa, come with me."

"What is to be done?" asked the President of Annie.
"You know her best.  What if I compel her to stay?  Would
there be danger?"

"I think she would probably die to-night, as she says.  If
she could convince herself of her weakness, that would be
best.  She cannot walk to the shore.  She cannot sit in an
open boat in winter weather."

"You are right.  I will let her try.  She may endure
conviction by such means."

"I will go with you to help her home."

"That is well; but you are feeble yourself."

"I am, sir; but I must try what I can do."

Lady Carse was over the threshold within the ten minutes,
followed by Helsa with a bundle of clothes.  She cast a
glance of fiery triumph back at the dwelling, and round the
whole desolate scene.  For a few steps she walked firmly,
then she silently accepted the President's arm.  Further on,
she was glad to have Helsa's on the other side.

"Let me advise you to return," said the President, pausing
when the descent became steeper.  "By recruiting here till
the spring, you——"

"I will recruit elsewhere, thank you.  When I once get
into the boat I shall do very well.  It is only this steep
descent, and the treacherous footing."

She could not speak further. All her strength was required to keep herself from falling between her two supporters.

"You will not do better in the boat. You mistake your condition," said the President. "Plainly, my conviction is, that if you proceed you will die."

"I shall not. I will not. If I stay, I shall not see another day. If I go, I may live to seventy. You do not know me, my lord. You are not entitled to speak of the power of my will."

The President and the widow exchanged glances, and no further opposition was offered.

"We may as well spare your strength, however," said the President. "The boatmen shall carry you. I will call them. Oh! I see. You are afraid I should give you the slip. But you may release my skirts. Your servants will do us the favour to go forward and send us help."

The boatmen looked gloomy about conveying two women —one of them evidently very ill; and Sir Alexander would have refused in any other case whatever. But he had vowed to interfere no more in Lady Carse's affairs, but to consider her wholly the President's charge.

"I see your opinion in your face," said the President to him, "and I entirely agree with you. But she is just about to die, at all events; and if it is an indulgence to her to die in the exercise of a freedom from which she has been debarred so long, I am not disposed to deny it to her. I assume the responsibility."

"My doubt is about the men," observed Sir Alexander; "but I will do what I can."

He did what he could by showing an interest in the embarkation of the lady. He laid the cloaks and plaids for her in the bottom of the boat, and spoke cheerfully to her—almost jokingly—of the uncertainty of their destination. He lifted her in himself, and placed Helsa beside her; and then his men dared not show further unwillingness but by silence.

Lady Carse raised herself and beckoned to Annie. Annie leaned over to her, and said,

"Dear Lady Carse, you look very pale. It is not too late to say you will come home with me."

Lady Carse tried to laugh; but it was no laugh, but a convulsion. She struggled to say,

"I shall do very well presently, when I feel I am free. It is only the last prison airs that poison me. If we never meet again——"

"We shall not meet in life, Lady Carse. I shall pray for you."

"I know you will. And I—I wished to say—but I cannot——"

"I know what you would say. Lie down and rest. God be with you!"

All appeared calm and right on board the boat, as long as Annie could watch its course in the harbour. When it disappeared behind a headland, she returned home to look

"IT IS NOT TOO LATE TO SAY YOU WILL COME HOME WITH ME."

for it again. She saw it soon, and for some time, for it coasted the island to the northernmost point for the chance of being unseen to the last possible moment. It was evidently proceeding steadily on its course, and Annie hoped that the sense of freedom might be acting as a restorative for the hour to the dying woman. Those on board hoped the same; for the lady, when she had covered her face with a handkerchief, lay very still.

"She looks comfortable," whispered the President to Sir Alexander. "Can you suggest anything more that we can do?"

"Better let her sleep while she can, my lord. She appears comfortable at present."

Three more hours passed without anything being observable in Lady Carse, but such slight movements now and then as showed that she was not asleep. She then drew the handkerchief from her face and looked up at Helsa, who exclaimed at the change in the countenance. The President bent over her, and caught her words—

"It is not your fault—but I am dying. But I am sure I should have died on land, and before this. And I have escaped! Tell my husband so."

"I will. Shall I raise you?"

"No; take no notice. I cannot bear to be pitied. I will not be pitied; as this was my own act. But it is hard——"

"It *is* hard : but you have only to pass one other threshold courageously, and then you are free indeed. Man cannot harm you there."

"But, to-day, of all seasons——"

"It *is* hard : but you have done with captivity. No more captivity ! My dear Lady Carse, what remains ! What is it you would have ? You would not wish for vengeance ! No ! it is pain !—you are in pain. Shall I raise you ? "

"No, no ; never mind the pain ! But I did hope to see my husband again."

"To forgive him. You mean, to forgive him ? "

"No ; I meant——"

"But you mean it now ? He had something to pardon in you."

"True. But I cannot——Do not ask me."

"Then you hope that God will. I may tell him that you hope that God will forgive him."

"That is not my affair. Kiss my Janet for me."

"I will ; and all your children—— What ? 'Is it growing dark ?' Yes, it is, to us as well as to you. What is that she says ? " he inquired of Helsa, who had a younger and quicker ear.

"She says the widow is about lighting her lamp. Yes, my lady ; but we are too far off to see it."

"Is she wandering ? " asked the President.

"No, sir : quite sensible, I think. Did you speak, my lady ? "

"My love ! "

"To Annie, my lady? I will not forget."

She spoke no more. Sir Alexander contrived to keep from the knowledge of the boatmen for some hours that there was a corpse on board. When they could conceal it no longer, they forgot their fatigue in their superstition, and rowed, as for their lives, to the nearest point of land. This happened, fortunately, to be within the territories of Sir Alexander Macdonald.

In the early dawn the boat touched at Vaternish Point, and there landed the body, which, with Helsa for its attendant, was committed by Sir Alexander to a clansman who was to summon a distant minister, and see the remains interred in the church at Trunban, where they now lie.

When the President returned to his estate at Culloden, in the ensuing spring, on the final overthrow of the Jacobite cause, his first use of the re-established post was to write to Lord Carse, in London, tidings of his wife's death, promising all particulars if he found that his letter reached its destination in safety. The reply he received was this :—

"I most heartily thank you, my dear friend, for the notice you have given me of the death of *that person.* It would be a ridiculous untruth to pretend grief for it; but as it brings to my mind a train of various things for many years back, it gives me concern. Her retaining wit and facetiousness to the last surprises me. These qualities none found in her,

no more than common sense or good nature, before she
went to those parts ; and of the reverse of all which if she
had not been irrecoverably possessed, in an extraordinary
and insufferable degree, after many years' fruitless endeavours
to reclaim her, she had never seen those parts. I long for
the particulars of her death, which, you are pleased to tell
me, I am to have by next post."

" Hers was a singular death, at last," observed Lord
Carse, when he put the President's second letter into the
hands of his sister. " I almost wonder that they did not
slip the body overboard, rather than expose themselves to
danger for the sake of giving Christian burial to such a
person."

"Dust to dust," said Lady Rachel, thoughtfully. "Those
were the words said over her. I am glad it was so, rather
than that one more was added to the tossing billows. For
what was she but a billow, driven by the winds and
tossed? "

When, some few years after, the steward approached the
island on an autumn night, in honour of Rollo's invitation
to attend the funeral of the Widow Fleming, his eye unconsciously sought the guiding light on the hill side.

" Ah !" said he, recollecting himself, " it is gone, and we
shall see it no more. Rollo will live on the main, and this
side of the island will be deserted. Her light gone ! We
should almost as soon thought of losing a star. And she
herself gone ! We shall miss her, as if one of our lofty old

rocks had crumbled down into the sea. She was truly, though one would not have dared to tell her so, an anchorage to people feebler than herself. She had a faith which made her spirit, tender as it was, as firm as any rock."

THE END.

www.ingramcontent.com/pod-product-compliance
Lightning Source LLC
Chambersburg PA
CBHW030809020726
47499CB00006B/1831